ROD DAMON IS UP AGAINST THE CUTEST ENEMY AGENTS IN THE WORLD!

The Coxeman comes to Paris to search the pleasure houses of that most pleasurable of all cities for some dangerous-but-beautiful lady-spies who have been playing havoc with the delegates to the Paris peace talks.

Rod's attack must be strong enough to overcome the spies' depraved techniques or the high-level talks will peter out, and the biggest sex-scandal the Free World has ever known will come to a head.

Can Rod stay abreast of all the intrigue?

COXEMAN #14

A GOOD PEACE

AN ADULT NOVEL BY BY TROY CONWAY

POPULAR LIBRARY

Copyright © 1969 by Coronet Communication, Inc.
All rights reserved. Except as permitted under the U.S. Copyright Act of 1976, no part of this publication may be reproduced, distributed, or transmitted in any form or by any means, or stored in a database or retrieval system, without the prior written permission of the publisher.

Popular Library
Hachette Book Group USA
237 Park Avenue
New York, NY 10017

Popular Library is an imprint of Grand Central Publishing. The Popular Library name and logo is a trademark of Hachette Book Group USA, Inc. The Coxeman name and logo is a trademark of Hachette Book Group USA, Inc.

Visit our Web site at www.HachetteBookGroupUSA.com

First Paperback Printing: July, 1969

Printed in the United States of America

Conway, Troy
Good Peace, A / Troy Conway
(Coxeman, #14)

ISBN 0-446-54319-5 / 978-0-446-54319-4

CHAPTER ONE

It all started with a thesis, a white feather and a French lesson. Not exactly in equal parts but relatively interesting and exciting. That's the way it usually is with theses, white feathers and French lessons.

The thesis (to take them in order) was a neatly typewritten school paper submitted to me by one Danielle Lebeau of Paris, dealing with those aspects of academic knowledge which had fascinated me longer than any other aspect of my life. To wit: sexology. Or rather the psychology of sexology. Of which, I, Rod Damon, head of the League for Sexual Dynamics, now am considered the foremost mind (and body) in the field.

The white feather had come off a duck's South end and became a titillating weapon between the beautifully lush red lips of a Polynesian exchange student named Minda Loa. But more of that anon.

The French lesson was the *piece de résistance* at the very end of a long hot summer evening. But that too comes later. By the time I had mastered my French, not even De Gaulle could have stopped me. This French had a Polynesian translation.

But first things first. Miss Danielle Lebeau's intriguing thesis: *Sex and Concentration.*

There I was, wearing nothing but my skin, ensconced in my professorial quarters at the university, poring over students' papers. In my celebrated role as Master and Scientist, it was my sworn duty and pleasure to assist young minds the world over in their search for knowledge and truth about sex and mores and morals. Miss Lebeau's paper became such fascinating reading that I curled up in the altogether behind my desk, warmed only by a briar pipe and my natively torrid nature. I am never really ever very cold. I'm young, handsome and well-hung. Somewhere amidst the union of these fine three endowments lies complete warmth of physical body.

Miss Lebeau's thesis, some forty-five pages of closely bunched type and text, bore a Paris address. That too intrigued me at first. French ladies are extremely curious about their sexual instincts, as any reader of Françoise Sagan surely knows. But not even little sad Françoise ever had any notions like Miss Danielle Lebeau.

I became immediately rapt on page one of the thesis and read on, puffing furiously at the briar pipe. The lady, whoever she was, didn't have a drop of *tristesse* in her make-up.

". . . . *no matter how the male of the species is occupying himself (bowling, working at the mill, starving to death or even dying!) he is always capable of being aroused sexually. His primary drive and/or need to propogate himself seems to take precedence over every other human function. When his sexual arousal is in progress, it supercedes any other need. Indeed, he will pay no attention to a burning building or the screams of a fellow human in distress. In effect, the male animal must be sated before he does anything else. . . ."*

That gave me pause. The French mademoiselle, whoever she was, was very close to the carnal truth. Fifty million Frenchman could not be wrong but despite her brilliance, her eternal verities, her daring thinking, she had erred. Probably the girl was very young. What other explanation could there be for the simple fact that she didn't know that while sexual arousal may very well be the drive of drives, and the one that consumes all concentration and effort until fulfillment, conversely, any form of fear or shock could wipe out the feeling in a flash. A woman wouldn't succumb that way because of her lack of phallus but after all, men were the subject of Miss Lebeau's thesis and she ought to realize that the biggest erections in the world had vanished in a twinkling because the husband came home when he was least expected; or the hungry male, bent on penetration, suddenly hears the door to the bedroom being broken down by a battery of private detectives; and the like. No, Miss Lebeau could not know. Therefore she was young. Her thesis was brilliant and generally correct but she had not allowed for the facts of life.

There were many other estimable facets to her thesis and when I had done, I reached for a ball point pen to register some marginal comments on her paper.

6

It was while I was pondering how best to reject Miss Lebeau's paper without nipping a budding sexologist's enthusiasm altogether, that the feather intruded on my consciousness.

That feather.

The apartment was air-conditioned, the carpet pile very pleasurable on my bare feet and the room temperature superb. I always lived first class at the university since my remarkable career had put the place on the map, swelling the rolls with eager young coeds anxious and willing to learn the ancient sexual customs and mores I had presented to the world on a plate way back at the beginning. But not even a comfortable den-office could account for the simple fact that the hairs on the back of my neck were suddenly rising. Unfurling, as it were. I froze in my chair, a swivel-seated leather masterpiece of comfortable design.

An insanely tickling sensation was traveling up the naked flesh of my body, beginning at the toes of my feet. A light, almost spidery touch was wafting gently over my skin. Then my nostrils, my ears, even my soft palate began to itch uncontrollably. For a long, delicious moment, every atom of my body was alerted. Ready for the boudoir, as it were. Every inch of me was throbbing with new-found desire.

I am not *allergic* to anything; neither am I an idiot.

I reached down into the recess of the area between the sides of my desk. My fingertips brushed against something soft, textured like velvet and indubitably female. With a happy sigh, I pushed the swivel chair back and looked under the desk.

It was then that I saw the great white feather.

I am not a movie star nor the richest man in the world, financially that is, but I am no stranger to the pursuit of lovely women the world over, eager to learn what makes Rod Damon tick.

It was Minda Loa.

She was an olive-skinned, straight-haired and incredibly endowed exchange student. She was crouched on her shapely dark knees, her curvaceous face tilted up to me. Between her white teeth, a duck's white feather stuck out like an arrow. It was this weapon of pleasure with which

7

she had 'feathered' my prop, as it were. Using it to brush upwards from my toes until its light maddening touch had converted my testes into a Dante's Inferno of excitement. Never mind the Chinese. The Pacific ain't so bad either when it comes to instruments of desire.

When she saw me she frowned, but her teeth never let go of the feather. And her red lips drew back in a worried grimace.

"Oh, Master, may I please?"

"As you were," I growled.

I am ever ready for new explorations, new wonders to recount to my fellow man. It is my sworn duty to the science of research and sexology. A white duck feather was a famous first for me, as innocuous as that may seem.

"If only I may please you . . ."

"Please me."

"It is seldom that Minda Loa has had a chance to be alone with you. The classroom is so crowded . . ."

"Mmmmm," I said.

"And I have so much to share with you. And tell you. And ask you."

"Your lips are moving but I can't hear a word you're saying." I closed my eyes and sat back in the chair. "Teach me."

She stopped talking. I heard a light little giggle, a compound of happiness and eagerness, and she was off to the races.

She knew what to do with the feather, all right. My Polynesian research notes and statistics tell me that the feather touch custom is as popular as pineapples in the South Seas. Once a formal rite among the priests and priestesses of the ancient civilization, it is now something even the natives can get restless about. And they do. Small wonder. As a sensory, excitatory thrill, it can drive you up the wall. I felt like the Five Little Peppers. I grew and grew and grew. Each tiny, separate hair of my body was being kissed.

Minda Loa knew her stuff. She was the dark and roving kind.

The Polynesians never used the tongue, only the feather, but earlier in the week during some private instruction I had showed her just what she and the crowd back home

8

were missing. Still, she wanted to make a point, I guess. The feather had a lot going for it. It was just like the daring minx to sneak into my study to get some of her own back. Yet, for all of that, she was a Damon devotee, an acolyte, a camp follower. The feather suddenly fluttered against my knee on its was down to the floor. And then her red lips closed over me and I closed my eyes even tighter. The body's most versatile sexual stimuli, manipulated by Minda Loa, is not a weapon to sneeze at. And I don't mean the feather.

Her hot, liquid-like tongue laved me. And laved and laved and laved. I was at full mast now, thanks to her divine feather, and as her lips bit home, she placed her hands against the seat of the swivel chair and moved it back another foot so she'd have more room to breathe. Then slowly, with infinite care and patience, and all the skill there is, her tongue darted and licked. Licked and flicked all over me, burning and soothing at one and the same time. Fire and ice. What a combination. In ten minutes flat, I could have easily been accused of having grown a third leg.

I opened my eyes once to study her, to savor the splendor of her passion. As the girls go, she was a volcano.

In the Trader Vic league, she would have to rate a prize pineapple. But they never found specimens like her on Easter Island. She was the Polynesian bunny of your fondest fantasies.

Picture a little more than ninety pounds of proportionate female, maybe no more than four feet ten inches in height, but curvy and sensuous down to her naked instep. She had firmly round hips, flowering out to a small waist. Her bosom, albeit small by the standards of Italian films, were as matchingly symmetrical and globular as prime Florida oranges. Her Venus mound was a streamlined mat of silken dark hair and even as she pumped and gyrated below me on her knees, it was enticing to behold and wonder about. A superb resting place for the joy toy of the world. I began to get restless. She sensed that and redoubled her suckling. Every movement, clockwise, counterclockwise, was stirring me to heights that it seemed even I had never before attained.

"Ah, Master . . ."

9

"Mmmmm?"

"You are the tallest man in the world . . . my God."

"If you say so."

I was feeling too good to argue. Her fiery mouth had scorched me. I was on fire, burning from toe to crown. Did you ever have the feeling that you were *never* going to go down?

I couldn't get too comfortable in the swivel chair. It was like a bower of flowers, all swimming in velvet and satin and silk. I was floating, buoyed by the devilish red mouth with the fierce pink tongue which had drawn forth every atom of my being. I kept my eyes closed. It felt twice as good. Feathers are fine for ducks and all sorts of winged life, but give me the gift of tongues any time, chums.

"Minda . . ."

"Yes?"

"You're biting me now . . ."

"Oh . . . forgive me . . . it is just that the sweetness of thy flesh carried me away. . . ."

"Sure."

"I'm sorry."

"All is forgiven."

And that alone makes Walrus-moustache, my friend and employer from the Thaddeus X. Coxe Foundation, which underwrites all my research projects while also using me as a Master Spy of sorts, positively livid with envy.

"*Aloha,*" I said feebly, trying to keep from grabbing her by the shoulders and hoisting her onto my manhood. Rushing spoils things. You must never rush. Didn't that old eighth century Arab swinger, Jalal al-Din al-Siyuti, always claim: *Do not make haste in the establishment of conjugal action?* The old tent sexologist had been a better man than I was, Gunga Din. My first God in my studies; he never failed. At the least, his maxims and rules never did.

Minda Loa misunderstood me. Her mouth left the family jewels, and traveled easily down toward my knees. I laughed and this time I did reach down and pull her up to me. Her dark eyes glowed with happiness at my touch. She shuddered ecstatically and her oranges fell off the shelf. I caught them before they could get away completely.

"What do you want of me, Master?"

10

"Guess."

"This?" She straddled my thighs, flinging one superb leg across me.

"Could be."

"And this?" The other leg scissored out so that she was posed just behind the towering flag of the compound. I hesitated only one second longer, drinking in the lovely architecture of her body, sitting me as if she was about to ride a horse.

"You're getting warmer," I said.

She laughed in a low monotone and eased herself gently atop me.

The Venus mound rested easily for another second, barely touching the tip of me, and then her eyeballs disappeared and her slender exquisitely rounded little body settled down for a long stay. Contact was explosive, sudden and a pinwheeling madness of movement and color, all accompanied by low-voiced moans and whimpers of ungovernable desire and satisfaction.

She became a yo-yo, a moving vessel of erotica. I let her have full rein for only minutes and then I took over. She was greasing the pole, swallowing it up in that dark interior that makes every woman the same and yet every woman different. But I have my own ego and it demands giving every woman that joins me the thrill of a lifetime. That's not such a bad *raison d'etre* for a man's existence, is there?

Minda Loa didn't think so.

She shot out one long, loud moan as the shaft struck the richest oil deposit in the human book. Even working from beneath her, I had her hoisted to the very ceiling of the study, spearing her with all the tact, delicacy and deliberation at my command. Endless seconds raced by, counterpointed by her gyrating flesh, my thrusting pokes toward Mecca and with it all, Minda Loa, forgetting all about feathers and tongues and Polynesia, let me know in very explicit bedroom language just how much she was enjoying getting her ashes hauled.

I seldom talk during coitus but the women always do. Possibly the by-products of the Victorian age we still live in, for all of the so-called freedoms. *The* woman still wants *the* man to think she is something sweet and

11

feminine and soft. A deception very ill-advised for the proper enjoyment of love games. Ask any psychiatrist. Freud had his nose to the right grindstone, all right. The completely uninhibited woman still has the best time in bed. Bar nobody.

"Ah, Master . . . that is so big and round and nice. I feel as if you are stuffing me with a mango tree and the tree is full of chattering, playful monkeys all running around among the branches and leaves. Ohhhhhhh . . . Popocapattakeetle . . . !"

She mispronounced it but what the hell. I wasn't humming along with her pagan tunes because she had perfect diction. The point is she thought *I* had and as always, that is very good enough for me.

I had forgotten all about Danielle Lebeau's very interesting thesis, now lying abandoned on the floor where the wind of Minda Loa's up-and-down flurry of body had blown it to the carpet.

Fire and ice, suction and succulence. Little Minda Loa was a poem of passion. A pearl of the Pacific. I wondered what island chain had gotten her so keyed up. Her olive face was a fiery mask of exotica now, despite the tears of joy flooding her eyes. But her mastery and complete cooperation and abandon had sucked out the marrow of my bones and turned me to jelly.

She collapsed on my stomach. I sagged back in the swivel chair. Our boiling bodies were plastered together like two strips of flypaper. There was that exceedingly rich, delightful dampness of our bodies that so clearly is the evidence of a happy time.

"Again?" she whispered softly in my ear.

"Don't you ever get tired?"

"Not with you, Master. And dare you call the kettle black when your pot yet smolders?" Okay, it was true. As sated as I was, the old divining rod was as amiably stout and solid as ever. Just a trifle subdued around the edges.

"You're right. Tell you what. Since I'm your teacher and you have a real thirst for knowledge, perhaps I can extend your knowledge. Have you ever tried the Kentucky Runaway?"

She raised herself above my chest, staring into my eyes.

"Kentucky . . . ?"

"Yes. It's an American custom that is surprisingly advanced for an area of such slight cultural advantages. But you'll like the method. All we need is us and some room. Plenty of room to move. It's quite simple. You pretend to be the horse and I'm your rider. Of course, I don't get on top of you but rather I stand behind you and when I say Gallop! you try to run ahead of me without my being able to reach you—of course, you can't duck or dodge. You just keep on the straightaway. Trying to run away, see? I try to head you off. From the rear. It's a truckload of fun."

Her eyes glowed eagerly.

"Don't you ever reach the limit of your inventiveness, Master?"

"Pshaw. I've got a million of them—"

"Don't you ever quit?"

That wasn't Minda Loa walking and I did not have to look up from my chair to see who had barged in on me for the nine thousandth time at the wrong time. Walrus-moustache has an absolute genius for finding me in the buff with some woman. He's not a *voyeur* or queer in any way, you understand, it is simply that he is Bad News, Incorporated.

As a front for the Thaddeus X. Coxe Foundation, which presumes to pose as a group of Right Wing America Firsters, he is also the man who dishes out the espionage assignments that have come very close to getting me killed. In case you haven't heard, I am the James Bond of the sex world.

I closed my eyes. I didn't want to see the supercilious smirk of his trim, classic face. He always came complete with bowler hat, dark clothes and the smirk. And an eternal satisfaction in cutting short my homework.

"Tut, tut, Damon . . ." I heard him say.

"I have no desire to discuss dead Egyptian kings with you," I said, still with my eyes closed. "Please take off. Make like a ballerina and dance away."

Minda Loa left my lap. I had to open my eyes. I rocked down in the swivel until my bare feet held the floor. She was quite an exchange student. I think she would have exchanged anything. She had moved swiftly across the floor, genuflected at the feet of Walrus-moustache until her but-

13

tocks were a perfect eight. My employer merely coughed brusquely and stared down at her.

"Does the divine man with the moustache," Minda Loa cooed in her mellow voice, "wish to make love also?"

"Certainly not!" Walrus-moustache harrumphed, twirling his scrubby hirsute adornment.

Minda Loa raised herself, turned to me, bowed and then without so much as a Bye, Bye, Baby, pattered out of the room. Her buttocks shimmered as she walked. The long dark hair trailed; her shoulders sagged, however.

When the door closed, I yawned.

"You hurt her feelings," I said.

"She made me nervous. Make love. The idea."

"I'm glad she made you nervous. Maybe it will cure you of this terrible habit you have of catching me flagrante delicto."

His eyebrows rose and he stepped further into the room. His eyes swept over my male equipment and he sniffed again. Out of deference to his internal envy, I moved closer to the desk so that half of me was hidden from view. The important half.

"Odd you should use that expression, Damon. It has all to do with what has brought me flying to your very doorstep once again. Truly, I could well believe in ESP."

"Tell it to Sweeney. Any man who wears a belt and suspenders and carries safety pins doesn't believe in anything."

He scowled and ignored the remark, taking the soft plush chair on the other side of the desk. He could still see my undercarriage so he shifted his chair, still scowling.

"Damon, we must talk. I've locked the door—"

"I wish I had."

He wagged his head. "I have never known a man like you. By my estimate you have had at least one woman every day of your life since your college studies and experiments launched you into the limelight. By thunder, man, I'm probably underestimating the count!"

"Is there any other way to live?" I reached for my pipe and relit it. I puffed on it and he sighed unhappily.

"The Foundation needs your services once again. Now, don't regale me with your familiar complaints and fears.

14

We've been through all this before. You're still the best man we have for any field work that entails sexual activity. Agreed?"

"Agreed. What now, my love?"

"I am not your love and since I never intend to take that circuitous route, we won't discuss it at all."

"You're so right. When it comes to that, you can go screw yourself."

"Please, Damon." He looked miserable. "Must we? Always you offer me this wit and rebuff, and in the end, you do the job anyway and have a high old time. Do you remember Berlin? Mexico? Sarmania? You got enough research data out of those countries to stock the New York Public Library, the London Museum and, yes, the Smithsonian Institute! Not to mention the National Archives. Do let me get on with it."

"Get on with it, then. It's past my bedtime."

"No, my friend. You will pack a bag, two bags if you have to, and sleep on the night plane to Paris. We have another big one for you. As always, perhaps the biggest one so far." His caustic gaze searched my face. "Have you been following the peace talks?"

"I follow that all the time. You know me. Piece at any price."

"Damon! Stop joking, man. I'm discussing something that is no laughing matter. No place to make puns or bantering remarks. Really, Damon——"

"All right. Relax." I put the pipe down, folded my arms and leaned back in the swivel chair. In spite of his being there, I felt like a million dollars, all in negotiable bonds. Minda Loa had made my evening. Not even Walrus-moustache and his categorical imperatives could sour that for me. "What's bothering the Thaddeus X. Coxe Foundation—and this dreary old automated world of ours —now?"

Walrus-moustache stiffened. The way he usually does when he's about to drop a bomb in my lap. Naked or otherwise.

"The safety of the free world, Damon."

"Oh, that old thing—"

"World peace, Damon," he said grittingly between his
15

teeth, "and your inalienable right to go on screwing to your heart's desire. Does that interest you, my dear fellow Coxeman?"

I lost my cool. Anything that affects or can affect that—change my way of happy living—had to be important. I put a serious expression on my face to mollify him and paid closer attention. He was heartened by my response and lost some of his own cynicism and biting tongue.

"Wow," I said. "All that? What could be so bad that it might do all those terrible things you said?"

"The Paris peace talks," Walrus-moustache said with dreadful emphasis. "Someone is out to wreck them. To sabotage them, to kill them. You know what that means? If peace talk fails at this dangerous time, the whole world could go to war. You know what that means?"

"Yeah. They use the bomb, we use the bomb and nobody will be around to tot up the score."

"Precisely. And now I'll explain it all to you so that you will know why it is so imperative that you fly to Paris as soon as possible. You should have been there *yesterday*, old boy."

"I get the picture. Start talking. The sooner the better."

I gave him a break. I put a bathrobe on and made some coffee while he poured out the sad, important, wretched news about the state of the world.

Something wasn't only rotten in Paris; it was lousy in every spot on the globe. The Coxeman Foundation was worried. And when they worry, Rod Damon swings into action. Once again, the die was cast. I was going to be asked to give more than my life for my country.

Once again I was very much wanted.

Balls and all.

You'd be amazed, really, just how many of the espionage, foreign intrigue *cum* security problems of this mad old universe have been solved, avoided or gotten around via the bedroom. Sex is perhaps the greatest secret weapon in the business. Ask the CIA, ask Interpol, ask the FBI, but above all, ask the Coxe Foundation. Sometimes a dame with measurements of 38x22x38 can stop a hydrogen bomb from going off if some mad scientist has a restless liver. No specifications on a drawing board can

16

ever match the arsenal of one torrid tomato out to make or break a code or steal a blueprint or make a genius defect to the enemy. As for the male spy—*great!*

And if one secret agent, very well hung, properly spirited and loaded with charm, is on your side, why, then you can steal a march on all the would-be Napoleons and budding Eva Perons in the political grab-bag.

The Coxe Foundation has always found it so.

I, Rod Damon, am their secret weapon.

And they sure know how to use me.

CHAPTER TWO

Walrus-moustache settled down for a nice long chat. I made myself comfortable behind the desk. Gone but not forgotten was Danielle Lebeau's fascinatingly incorrect thesis. It still lay on the floor between us. Walrus-moustache had sniffed down at the clutter only once as if to rebuke me for disorderliness but immediately got back to the business at hand. The coffee on the stove bubbled merrily, filling my rooms with the wonderful aroma of fresh java. Somewhere on the campus grounds, a clock tolled ten times. The night was still young.

"Take it from the top," I suggested. "The peace talks are important. I know that. So who's spoiling the party? Moscow?"

He shivered. "That could be. They would like to see China busy in Asia, would like the war to continue. But a world holocaust wouldn't fit into their next ten-year plan right now, I would say."

"China, then?"

"Possibly. They do want the U.S.A. hot and bothered at all times. Anything that drains our economy, such as the war effort, would make them ecstatic. But again—it's hard to say for sure."

"How about the United Arab Republic?"

"No, Damon." Walrus-Moustache winced. "It's true our new man in the White House is committed to help Israel and if the Viet Nam thing ends, we certainly would have more time and more money to aid Israel, but again, the Arabs are merely a possible bad man in this project."

"You sure aren't making it easy," I said. "Can it be that some notoriously Right Wing Yankee-Doodle-Not-So-Dandies are trying to louse things up? Just out of sheer blindness and stupidity?"

Walrus-moustache spread his manicured hands and smiled sourly. His eyes were appreciative. He likes it when I know my politics.

"You have put forth some excellent candidates for troublemaking, Damon. But let me clue you in. Right

18

now, the guilty nation would be anybody's guess. After all, ostensibly, the whole world is in on the peace talks. Even France has a stake. As well as our British friends and the lesser nations such as Italy and Spain." He leaned forward in his chair and his right shoe brushed against Danielle Lebeau's thesis. He ignored it. "As of yesterday, a sex scandal has broken all over Paris. Involving one of the very officials sitting in for France. Gaston Corbeau's mistress or personal acquaintance or secretary or what have you, was knifed in the left breast with an Oriental dagger. The woman is dead, of course, and all Paris is talking about her affair with a man so highly placed in government. Corbeau is married, you see, and the dead woman, a Miss Danielle Lebeau, seems to have been a member of the *Académie Sexualité*—you should appreciate that, my dear Damon. It's a woman's college devoted to *your* main interest in life. But to get on with it—whatever the woman was she somehow left a coded message for the Coxe Foundation satisfied that Gaston Corbeau is a victim of unfortunate circumstances. After all, many an influential man gets to know a beautiful woman but you know the French; they are smacking their chops over this one. It's—ah—extremely *juicy*. Miss Lebeau was a stunning brunette. Only twenty-one. Corbeau is over sixty. You see how it is. There may be no connection with Miss Lebeau's demise and the peace talks—*except* for the nature of the message which we decoded and I now have in my pocket." He reached into his impeccable coat and drew forth a folded tissue-like streamer of paper, passing it across to me. I took it, my mind agreeing with what he said about ESP. How many women living in Paris could be named Danielle Lebeau who went to academies for sexual study and wrote theses like the one that now lay on the floor of my college home!

"Lebeau," I said. "What was she doing in the *Académie Sexuality*?"

"Working for her Ph. D. Do you know her?"

"Only by mutual interest. Pick up that thesis on the floor and don't call me a hoodoo. It's a helluva coincidence."

While he was snorting in amazement over the by-line typed on the cover of the thesis, I scanned the note. It was in block letters, all caps and had obviously been transcribed from its original form by some Coxeman underling in the office:

I HAVE REFUSED TO WORK FOR THEM. THEY WISH ME TO INVOLVED THE ADVISORS IN A TRAP WHERE THE WORLD WILL REJECT THE PEACE EFFORTS. THREE MEN AND ONE WOMAN AND MEMBERS OF THE ACADEMY WILL BE CAUGHT FLAGRANTE DELICTO. SEE DANIELLE.

(signed) DANIELLE

When I looked up, Walrus-moustache was almost glaring at me. I shrugged.

"Don't chew my head off. I never met the woman. She sent me her thesis because we lend-lease our professional talent here. I also read theses by overseas students. I don't know Danielle Lebeau from Danielle Darrieux."

"Extraordinary." He sniffed again. "I come to you with a message sent to us—for you, by the way—from a woman soon to be murdered. What would make her think you were a spy as well as the eminent sexologist, Rod Damon?"

"I don't know."

"Think, man," he glowered. "You've had hundreds of women—no, thousand—had you ever met this Lebeau creature before?"

"Don't crowd me. I've had more women than you've had hot Sunday breakfasts, but offhand, no, I would honestly say I didn't know her. Not by that name, at any rate. Got a picture of her?"

He frowned. "Unfortunately, no. You'll have to find one of her in Paris somehow. Or go see the corpse."

"No, thank you. I'm a lover not a ghoul. Damn coincidence, isn't it? Me having the theseis, you having the message she wanted me to read."

"Yes," he growled. "And when I came in you used the very same expression she used in her decoded message. *Flagrante delicto.*"

"In my business," I sighed, "it's as normal as saying

20

'Had any lately?' Forget it. Question is—somebody must have tumbled to my cover. The fact that she knew she could reach me through the Coxe Foundation."

Walrus-moustache snorted. "Bah, forget that. We underwrite you, don't we? We pay for your research. Most natural thing in the world, I'd say." He riffled the pages of the thesis in his fingers. "Mind if I keep this for the time being? There's a bare possibility of more messages. Either between the lines or invisible ink. We'll fluoresce it and see what happens."

"I doubt that. That is merely a very potent, highly individual interpretation of sexual mores by a young woman out to make a point. But help yourself. It's Greek to me now. I'm more interested in what happens in Paris."

He nodded. "You see now, don't you, why you must go there at once? The woman's murder caused a scandal and any scandal however innocent could scuttle the whole project. Which is what we feel somebody certainly wants. Even among lesser officials, this sort of thing could blacken the eyes of the peace program. We can't have that, can we, now? You recall what the Profumo scandal did to the United Kingdom? It knocked the very bottom out of the English pound!"

"You're crazy," I laughed, "but I'll go. One of my fellow sexologists has been murdered, obviously, and even though she was a stranger, I feel I owe her the effort, at least. Who knows? Maybe it's just open season on sex scientists, and *that*, I am interested in. That could become a dangerous habit, knocking off people who want to find out all there is to know about sex. There's enough sexual ignorance in the world already."

"Damon," he said standing, "Coffee's done. May I have a cup?"

"Sure. Sorry I can't offer you even a stale doughnut or cruller. You see, sweets are very bad for the masculine potency factor, sugar has a tendency to——"

"Please, my dear fellow. Spare me your howling in the wilderness. I'll have my cuppa and then you will fly to Paris. As usual, the Coxe Foundation will allow you a very heavy expense account. I'm leaving you ten thousand dollars in American traveler's checks. As well as my Paris phone number. Again, caution is your byword and only call me when it's a life and death matter. Ostensibly, as the head of L.S.D., you can snoop around the *Académie Sexualité* to your heart's content. No one will question your interest. But it is up to you to find the connection between the Lebeau woman's murder and the peace talks. They've gone on a long time now and will probably continue past next Christmas, but as long as they *continue,* nothing must stop them. You will have to investigate and thwart this planned scandal which Miss Lebeau got wind of. Can you do all that, Damon?"

"Sure. I'm as bright as a pin. Did you know that the name *Corbeau* is the French word for *raven*?"

His eyes popped. "Incredible. And it means——?"

"Absolutely nothing. Just wanted to show you how bright I am and already I'm making like Sherlock Holmes. Jeezis, relax and sit tight, will you? Have the coffee before you explode."

An irritated smile crossed his face but he sat down, crossed his perfectly tailored knees and had a cup of my coffee. He sniffed at the vapors, nodded to himself and sipped. I looked at him and enjoyed my own cuppa knowing he would have preferred tea and that he hadn't removed his bowler hat in all the time he was in the room. He was a character, all right. My favorite bureaucrat. He would have been a perfect watchdog for a row of IBM machines. He had red tape in every one of his bloody veins.

"Oriental knife you said. Where?"

"In the left breast." He looked surprised.

"Get your dirty mind off sex. I mean—*where*?"

"Oh, sorry. In her own private room at the *Académie Sexualité*. Top floor back. Just overlooking the quadrangle. It's a large university. Almost as big as Fordham, say, in the Bronx, New York."

"How do they tie her in with Gaston Corbeau?"

He dabbed at his lips with his handkerchief after he set the coffee cup down on the desk. He saw the duck feather on the floor, reached down and picked it up, balancing it in the palm of his hand.

"The usual. Trysts remembered by other students. Miss Lebeau boasted of an admirer high in government. Someone else recalls the long Daimler with chauffeur appearing at the campus to pick her up on weekends. To cement the thing for the Paris police, Miss Lebeau had the usual tribute from an admirer. Fur coat, platinum cigarette case inscribed. Et cetera."

"Well, she lived it up before she died. That's something. What about her personal reputation?"

His eyes narrowed. "Amazingly contradictory, considering the externals. Her fellow students think of her as a Joan of Arc type. Refined, elegant, almost virginal. This affair with an older man seems to have been a recent thing. You will have to tread very carefully in that area, Damon. Corbeau is an influential man with many friends. Should you incur his wrath in any way, he can have you kicked out of France. Remember that."

"I will. Anything else to tell me before we kiss goodbye?"

"Yes." He held up the feather and waved it at me. "What in God's name is this doing here?"

"Duck feather. So what?"

He colored rapidly. "Dammit, are you taking to writing with a goosequill—er, duck quill?"

"No. That hot little number that walked out when you walked in is Minda Loa. In Polynesian circles, that feather is as artful an instrument as there is to excite male desire. Or female, for that matter."

"How?" He looked bewildered, the poor man. He never has understood my thirst for knowledge.

"I can't show you," I said primly, "and remain a heterosexual man. You see, Minda put the feather in her mouth and bent down before me in the altogether and gradually flicked the feather up and down all over my thighs until . . ."

"Please." His hands shot up. "Spare me the details. I may vomit."

"Spoilsport."

He stood up, brushed imaginary crumbs out of his lap and reset his iron bowler at a jaunty angle on his skull. His shrewd eyes appraised me with the usual quota of wonder and scorn.

"Damon, you are a shameless satyr. A cloven-hoofed, horned Sybarite who puts Petronius to the rear—"

"What, him too? Tsk, tsk."

23

"—and will go to his grave, if ever, as possibly the sole male cadaver in history with an erection. That is, if the autopsy people don't cut you off and pickle it in alcohol for the medical societies of the world."

"I love you too," I said.

"Go to Paris," he commanded. "Sow your usual oats but do well and Godspeed. As you know, we are behind you all the way."

"*Nobody* Greeks me."

"Damn you!" He sputtered and kept on sputtering until in all disgust he waved a defeated arm at me and shouldered out the door. I tried him at all times. But for peace at any price, he would put up with all the jibes, witticisms and corny comebacks I had to offer. Actually, he was a lot of fun to needle. I knew he was only a Victorian facade who had a night side that would be most revealing if any of his own bedroom peccadilloes were ever made public. Many was the time on an assignment when he rode the gravy train with me, scooping up whatever delicious morsels that fell his way. The damn prude. He was as horny as the next guy. *No,* hornier.

It was a night of revolving doors.

No sooner had the tall, trim bastard disappeared than the small, bountiful darling came back. Minda Loa came hurrying into the room, a filmy baby-doll fluttering around her like a pale cloud of stardust. She glowed, olive skin and all, with that beaming happiness that precedes a lot more happy times.

"He is gone, Master." Breathlessly, she came sweeping toward me on naked feet. In her hands were clasped a feathery pile of added duck weapons. "I came as soon as I could, knowing that you would want me to."

"You read my mind. Where were we?"

She giggled, slipping the baby doll down over her shapely shoulders until it was halted by her shapelier breasts. Her eyes laughed and she let the handful of feathers sail to the carpet.

"For later," she murmured. "Now, you must show me that Kentucky—what is it you called it?"

"Runaway. Not to be confused with the Georgia Gallop, the Texas Twister or the Pennsylvania Prance."

24

The baby-doll came to a rest around her knees. Her bronzed body glowed and she stepped toward me. A waft of perfume filtered across the atmosphere, getting a stranglehold on my nostrils. Man, she smelled good.

"I will be your mount," she whispered. "Do with me as you will; it is an honor."

"Turn around." I laughed. "Now bend forward. That's it. No, hold your hands back. They are the reins for me to hold. Now you just try to get away from me, Minda. Just try!"

She did as I told her. She took one last longing look at me over her shoulder. Her eyes were as big as Pacific moons. When she saw my riding crop, her whole body quivered with delight.

"Will you whip me, Master? *Please . . . ?*"

"That depends. Giddyap, Horsey!"

And away she went. With me not too far behind. Just close enough to let her feel the whip intermittently, just far away enough to keep her rotating, twisting *derriere* out of range until she was exhausted and couldn't and didn't want to get away anymore. She loved every lap of our race around the room, using the desk and one big chair as pylons and far turns. When I eventually flagged her down, it was right under the big windows that faced the campus proper. Only the full moon saw us.

What an exciting ride. Who needed a saddle?

A bareback excursion that left all previous memories and experiences in the barn. Minda Loa was a thoroughbred all the way and even though she wasn't born in Kentucky, or even raised in Georgia, I sure liked her peaches so she let me shake her tree. I'm mixing metaphors here but what the hell. She was eager, marvelous and tireless. So she wanted to find out about Texas and Pennsylvania and pretty soon we were working our way all across Rand-McNally. She loved every state in the union, up to and including Hawaii.

Along about six o'clock in the morning as the new sun spilled gold in through the windows, she shouted in delirum: "Five-Oh! Five-Oh! Master, we have accounted for every star!"

"And a few stripes too." There were lovely long scratch

25

marks all over my thighs where her nails had raked me with unbridled ecstasy. Her own tawny torso was a love map of bites and swollen kisses.

"Oh, Master. I call you that truly for I will be your slave forever. You have shown Minda Loa so much for her own thesis on lovemaking in the United States."

"I'm glad."

I really was but all night long and into the dawn, with the pile driver from Polynesia, I hadn't been able to remove from my mind the picture of a murdered student who had sent me a death message. Miss Danielle Lebeau.

The murdered mademoiselle had tainted all my fun and games, somehow. Damn Walrus-moustache and his blasted Coxe Foundation. Damn having to go to Paris. Damn having to leave great stuff like Minda Loa to play James Bond again. Sometimes, it just wasn't fair. Who the hell can really feel idealistic at dawn in the arms of a naked Goddess who doesn't know how to say No?

Believe me, it isn't easy.

When Minda Loa, who should have gone back to the dormitory hours ago, wriggled into her baby-doll and started for the door and then came back, waving a feather on the ball of her palm with that look in her eyes, who *could* have the heart to say, *"Beat it, baby. You've had enough!"*

I couldn't.

The sterner stuff I am made of is not that thing called Nobility or Self-sacrifice or Courage. Also, I should have been halfway to Paris.

"Master." Her arms went around my neck, she forced me down into the swivel chair again and she dropped to her knees, gently prying my thighs apart. "Let me blow you once more to the island of Paradise where the bird of love is always on the wing . . ."

There was only one bone left in my body.

"Be my guest," I muttered hoarsely. "Enjoy, enjoy . . ."

And so she did.

I loved Paris, I wanted to find the fiend or fiends responsible for the murder of Danielle Lebeau, I wanted to save the Peace Talks for the world and dear old Coxe

Foundation High, but as sure as they made dames and as sure as they made me to love them, Paris was going to have to wait.

No kid in the universe has ever parted with his 'horsey' with deeper regrets.

"Master."

"Now stop it. I got to get packed and get out of here. There's a plane I have to catch."

"Yes, yes. I will help you. But will you come back to Minda Loa? Promise me you will."

"Promises, promises. Tell you what. When I get back, which will probably be sometime before your final exams, I will show you a whole new thing about sex. "The Transylvanian Method. It's real weird."

"You will?" Once more, her arms and legs locked about me and the baby-doll was never going to stay on her. Her bronzed skin was glittering with the pearls of her passion. There was no surrender in the splendid young thing. In pure pagan terms, she was fantastic.

"I swear," I said.

Immediately her cool hands vised around the idol to whom she had yielded fealty for a good eight hours. Her dark eyes suddenly held all the wisdom in the world.

"Will you swear on *this* . . . that which is your very heart and soul?" Her ten supple fingers curled over the family jewels.

What could I do?

I swore.

It was only then that she left me to my packing, kissing me all the way to the last walk to the door. I felt like the love object of all time and I was firmly convinced I would have to toss out all my Polynesian research and start all over again. After all, Minda Loa had added a whole library full of addenda. Wowee.

"So long, Minda. Keep a sliced pineapple in the window for me."

"*Aloha,* Master." The poor kid was crying her eyes out. I was touched. "I can never forget what we shared this golden night."

When she left, finally, she was doing an impromptu *hula* in the corridor as she sashayed and flounced toward her own room. The quiet halls of the university building echoed with the slithering passage of her bared feet. Regretfully, I watched the finest fanny in the world disappear around the bend in the corridor. She was crooning some native ditty to herself and if it had been a rain dance, I think the whole sky would have opened up.

I was taking French leave from my studies but what the hell, I was my own boss, could write my own ticket. Let Walrus-moustache smooth out the details with the Faculty. As I was sure he had probably already done. He's no slouch when it comes to arranging things to suit his own ends.

I usually did all right in that department too.

My end was always well taken care of.

I'm like the Borgias in that respect, I guess,

The end *always* justifies my means.

A funny thing happened to me on the way off the campus. As I strode down the curving walks, bordered by a long line of elms, I was discovered in the act of departure by some of the fine young fillies from my lecture classes. They didn't need a guide book or a translation or an explanation. I had the look and manner of a man who was quitting the campus and it was too much for them.

Their voices blended in a universal wail of disappointment, which immediately transformed into a huge uproar of agony. Before I could smile away their fears or allay their suspicions with a trumped-up story about anything, they sprang for me, arms outstretched, skirts flying, tight sweaters juggling with offers. I started down the hill on the dead run with my suitcase firmly clasped under one arm. At any other time, such homage would have tickled the pants off me but who has time for about twenty hungry coeds at the break of day? I didn't. Minda Loa notwithstanding. I had to make that plane for Paris with something left over. And then some. Otherwise I wasn't going to do the Thaddeus X. Coxe Foundation a bit of good.

"Professor Damon, don't go . . . oh, you old meanie!!!!"

I knew them. All of them. Mary, Jennie, Jeanie, Irene, Samantha, Leona, Belle, Tonia, Sally . . . every one of them a poem, each a plum. But what the hell? There were lots more pebbles on the beach.

28

Down the hill they thundered after me. Screaming my name, crying out their wares, but it was hopeless. I had a fifty-yard start on them, and luckily a campus cab was waiting for me, flag up, motor purring.

I made it just in time, getting the door closed before they could touch me. The cab raced away, taking me from one form of university life toward the waiting world of another.

Little did I know, to coin a shopworn phrase.

CHAPTER THREE

The *Académie Sexualité* was a fooler, all right. It did not come as advertised by Walrus-moustache.

Only twenty-four hours after I planed out of the States, landed at Orly, and registered in a baroque hotel on the Champs de Renée about five hundred yards from the gurgling Seine—which has to be the dirtiest river in the world—I was trooping up the marble steps to the *Académie*. Walrus-moustache had described the place to a T. The quadrangle was as large as a football field and was flanked on all four sides by a low, two-storied Gothic structure that resembled a walled city. Like the Kremlin. The building was ugly terra-cotta with a somewhat modernistic gabled roof effect that was all wrong. A lot of green lawn and spreading chestnut trees dotted the corners of the quadrangle. The place looked like a temple of high learning. As academic as hell. One would never have expected the terra cotta barricaded a veritable army of panting, streamlined, mini-skirted broads from the outside world.

Paris was having a nice summer day. Blue skies, fleecy clouds and a squadron of sparrows chirping overhead. The quadrangle was sleepy and tranquil as my heels thumped along its marble corridors. Inside, the Académie was something else again. As I meandered among the wall paintings and marble busts of the likes of Freud, Henry Miller and Yankowski and Nabokov, my blood began to sing merrily in my veins. The dump was bursting at the gunwales with females. All sizes, shapes and colors. All wearing the same regulation dress of leather mini-skirt, white middie blouse with a daring V slash that went down as far as the buckled waist. The students wore psychedelic hose with patterns that would drive a Penny Arcade entrepreneur crazy. The girls, and they weren't all *jeunes filles,* were English, American, Latins, Orientals and Eurasians. Everybody had kind of a stainless steel look; despite the healthy display of bazooms, ample backsides, and red gashes for mouths and bouffant hairdos in all shades of the spectrum, nobody talked. There was a zombie-like, no-nonsense demeanor that prevailed. I walked among this horde of pulchritudinous knowledge-seekers and not one of them so much as looked to the left or right until I casually spoke my name aloud to another poised, shimmering creation sitting like God Almighty behind the Registration Desk.

Also, the marble corridors reeked, literally reeked, of an amalgam of exotic perfumes. Soft music, all string and ultra-sexual, seemed to emanate from the walls. Unobtrusive, erotic. Like *Night and Day* counterpointed with Ravel's *Bolero* with dashes of *Speak Low* and *Going Out of My Head Over You* thrown in.

The creature behind the desk looked up from the book she was reading. Red mouth, white teeth, peaches and cherries complexion and hair so taffied you'd want to eat it. She was chesty too.

"Oui, Monsieur?" she said evenly in clipped, precise schoolgirl French. She had America written all over her.

"Knock it off," I growled. "I'm Professor Damon from the United States. I want to see your head lady around here."

"Damon?" The taffy blonde's eyes started from their sockets. She forgot her book which turned out to be a dogeared copy of *Candy* and almost clapped her hands together. But her tremendous whim-whams got in the way. "Rod Damon?"

"One and the same. Heard of me, eh?"

"Oh, Professoooooooorrrrrrrr!" The French habit slipped out of her and she sat up higher in her chair, peering over the desk to look at my crotch. "Yes, yes, it is you! What are you doing here? To think—me, Mady Morrow from Chicago, should run across you like this! Oh, Professor, I think I've read *Linger Longer and Love It* over a dozen times—"

I run into this sort of thing all the time. It is embarrassing, even if it's heady stuff. I leaned across the desk.

"Please tone it down, Mady. You want to start a stampede? Just send me to your head lady and I'll come back, I swear, and you can tell me all about it. Okay?"

She shook her head vehemently, wiggled off her high

31

stool and came around the desk. She mashed up against me and began to rub like she had St. Vitus. Her red mouth reached up and bit my ear. Not hard, just painfully.

"No, you don't," she hissed. "You're the reason I enrolled in this high-priced joint. I'll take you to Madame personally. You're not going to slip out of my fingers—"

"I don't see how I can." It was true. Like so many true believers before her, she had to touch the miracle, feel it, weigh it in her hand. "If you're through now, let's go, huh?" I indicated the tall, sexy automatons sleepwalking past the desk on the way to their studies. She nodded quickly, winked, locked my arm in her own and practically dragged me down the marble corridor. She didn't seem to mind leaving the desk unattended. Nobody paid much attention to us. Maybe the rest of the dames thought she was doing her homework. After all, the *Académie Sexualité* was in existence solely to instruct females in the sexual arts. What a curriculum they must have had. I could almost see it: *"For tomorrow's lesson, you will sleep with one oversexed male and come back with a ten-page report on all that he says and does. And for the afternoon symposium on ménage à trois, each of you must tape-record all comments made during coitus. In this way, mademoiselles, we will learn much of the male animal and his sexual thresholds. . . ."* Open the door, Richard!

Mady Morrow was built like a carbon copy of Lillian Russell. Big, busty and a real dairy maid. She also had that gorgeous freedom of spirit that permits a girl to say everything and do everything without one squeamish second thought. She practically undressed me on the way to Madame's.

"Will you cut it out?" I slapped her hands way out of bounds. "Relax. Later but not now. This is important."

"Okay. But you take my room number. You memorize it, you don't forget it. Hot damn, this is a heaven-sent opportunity. I ball with you and I can kiss this *Académie* goodbye forever. I won't need any further instruction."

"Why? Isn't it fun here?"

"Ahhh. You can't get a man with a book. All the brains in the world can't make a man get the hots for you. Madame thinks so but Madame's a kook. You'll see. Here we are."

32

Before I could pursue that line of interesting investigation, she had goosed me so that I came slamming up against the door that said: *Madame de Jussac, Príncipe.* It was a steel door made to look like knotty pine. There was a gilded, embossed doorknob, right out of public school days. I felt a twinge of nostalgia. And then I felt Mady Morrow's right hand jarring my small intestine as she laughed happily in my ear.

"Man, are you put together! Mmmmmm . . . I'll wait right here."

"Aren't you going to announce me? Suppose she's doing an excercise with one of the students?"

"How did you guess? Go on. We all have permission to walk in anytime. She won't scream. This is the *Académie Sexualité, n'est pas?*" Her French was still atrocious. I said no more and escaped through the door. It swung on well-oiled hinging.

With Mady Morrow behind me and Madame De Jussac in front of me, I wasn't sure what to expect. Sort of Maria Ouspenskaya with a large gob of Marjorie Main and Anna Magnani thrown in but I'm no crystal ball expect. I was dead wrong.

The dame behind the plain chrome desk with glass top stepped out of my dreamland which is always peopled by the likes of Loren, Liz Taylor, Vera Miles and Kim Novak.

"Yes?"

"My name is Damon. Professor Red Damon. I hope you can give me some of your time."

"The Damon responsible for *The Fetish Encyclopedia* and all those volumes and treatises glorifying the carnal life? That Monsieur Damon?"

"Call me Rod. I'm a professor only to students."

"Welcome to *l'Académie Sexualité!* We are honored, Monsieur Rod."

"Thank you. Aren't you just a wee bit chilly, Madame?"

She should have been. She was naked from the waist up, placing on display a most magnificent set of female appendages. I had to get my bearings. On her and her office before I took another step into it. She was regarding me curiously from behind the desk, not answering my question, and obviously amused by it.

33

First of all, except for the desk—which didn't have so much as a blotter or pencil on it, only a French phone—the office was a bedroom. There were no file cabinets, no *éscritoires,* no nothing. Just the desk, four bare walls of nile green with French doors that opened on the quadrangle. And one bed. A bed of beds. Ever see one of those old movies where the queen is dying of something and maybe a dozen of the courtiers flock around to kiss her goodbye? That's the kind of four-postered, brocaded, monstrosity that spread out across the other half of the room, facing the window so that the morning sun could flood pure gold over the counterpane, delighting or annoying whoever was getting forty winks or forty kicks among the percales.

As for Madame de Jussac, pardon me while I catch my breath.

Her hair was red, flaming Maureen O'Hara red and it hung down her naked torso like a mantle of royalty. The splendid breastworks, twin howitzers aimed at me across the desk top, with two cherry-red areolas of unblinking majesty, neither sagged, flopped or jiggled. They might have been made of marble, so perfect was their texture and contour and mold. If I'd taken a tape measure I would have guessed they'd come out even down to the one millionth of a fraction. I hadn't seen such symmetry since my last glass of Balantine Beer. Her third ring was a seductive dimple of navel, as sensual as anything you could ever see. For toppers, the Madame's skin was pure ivory. No freckles or wrinkles or light smattering of gooseflesh. She was a sight for sore eyes. And definitely for well ones.

The legs crossed behind the desk thrust out like long guns from the abbreviated folds of another of those leather mini-skirts. I looked around the office for the matching middie shirt. It was draped on the bed. Pinned to the collar were two glittering medallions of some kind, catching the light of the sun. Unless I was nuts, they were the regulation oak leaf clusters of a major in the United States Army.

I didn't salute. I sat down in the chair in front of the desk. It was a red butterfly job that makes you sink almost out of sight. Sinking wasn't so bad. I could see up the creamy alley of her thighs. Torpedo Alley where all male projectiles ought to go someday. There was a tantalizing patch of darkness that clearly showed that Madame was not wearing any panties.

Madame de Jussac got up from behind the desk and came around it. A flicker of something had flashed in her eyes when she caught me eyeing her with obvious approval.

She walked like a major too, shoulders back, breasts out, but no major I ever met made me feel like she did. I wanted to trip her to the carpet, which was leopard-skin and about a foot thick, and twist her knobs until I got China, but I bided my time. I get around to all of them sooner or later. There was no hurry.

She loomed over my chair. Her eyes bored down at me. Her face was a chiseled masterpiece. So many inches of nose, red mouth and cheekbone. She had been chipped from the marble of men's dreams. Old Michelangelo would have cracked his hammer for her.

"So. You come to the *Académie Sexualité* and you disapprove of me at first sight. I suppose you will put that in your report to your Thaddeus X. Coxe Foundation?"

"Now, hold on. All I meant was—" I frowned. "The Coxe Foundation?"

"I know what you meant. Of course since they subsidize all that is here in the *Académie*, I cannot argue. But I assure you, Monsieur Damon. I have my reasons for going about—ah—topless, as you would say."

"I *would* say," I admitted, marveling at the devious brain of my employer and friend(?) Walrus-moustache. So the Coxe Foundation had footed the bill for the Academy. And he'd never told me. "And may I assure you your top is more not less. I'm delighted. No, I think they are swell. Point is—you must have a reason?"

She smiled and her icy tone dissolved.

"But of course! How else can I instruct these charming young girls in the matters of sexual education if I do not set them an example? I show them that a woman who is not ashamed of her gender will be proud to walk about, unimpeded, without hiding behind the garments of Victorian prudity. You see?"

"Yeah. Them that has them shows them. But why stop there? Why not go all the way?"

Her brows knit and then opened. "Ah! You mean in
35

total nudity? I tried that. Only last month. But you see, within these walls, without men here, it is quite harmless and all my girls enjoyed it. There was an outbreak of some lesbian overtures—to be expected—but that was nothing. I could handle that. But you see, we do get men on the premises. The delivery people—the butcher, the baker, the wigmakers, all those animals! Naturally they went berserk at sight of these splendidly developed young women. We had several cases of forcible rape but the ladies refused to press the charges. So naturally, I had to expel them from the school, to save the faculty from scandal."

"Oh, naturally."

"Yes. So thoroughgoing nudity poses a problem. However, I think if my ladies learn to walk about without shame, showing their breasts, they will assume a natural attitude about men. Then their studies will take on a new dimension. You for instance, of course, a man of your experience—do my breasts cause you any discomfort? Or is your blood quickening, the palms of your hands perspiring? But what am I saying? Merely uncross your legs, please."

I uncrossed them. A naughty smile swept across her beautifully perfect face. She wagged a finger at me and her breasts shifted just enough to convince me they were alive.

"Ah—I see they do effect you! I could hang my *chapeau* on that if ever I wore a *chapeau* and I do not."

"I," I said firmly, "am only human, and Madame is *tres* knockout."

"You are too kind."

"I'm all kinds. Wait and see."

She shrugged and the vital pair of mammaries danced. Still, she could not take her eyes off me. I would have tipped it for her if it had been a hat.

"Formidable!" she breathed.

"You can say that after you really get to know me better."

She arched her mouth at me. The eyes mocked me.

"My body pleases you, is that not so? You find it enticing?"

"Just a little around the edges, yes. Don't mind me. I always come to attention when in the presence of beautifully

36

endowed females. It's the tourist in me."

She didn't laugh. The green eyes were snaking up and down my full length. Madame must have seen plenty in her time, looking and thinking the way she did, but I was obviously something new under her sun. So I basked in some reflected glory.

I stared at her gorgeous shelf of treasures. It was simply incredible how well they matched, that gloriously symmetrical roundness and bold, vibrant fleshiness. Like two peas in a pod. Peas, hell! Balloons!

"Tell me something, Madame, if you will."

"It will be my pleasure, Monsieur Rod."

I shook my head. It was impossible to credit my eyes somehow. Just as she was so visibly impressed with my male artillery.

"I've often wondered," I said as light as I could. "Swinging loose and free like that and kind of bouncing around together, don't they ever get bruised or skinned or something?"

"Not in the slightest. Does that answer your question?"

"Uh—yes." I was disappointed. I must have sounded disappointed.

"Shall I replace my blouse?"

"You do and I'll knock you down. I'll live. This is my normal condition. It doesn't hurt at all."

"Really? How extraordinary. But then the man who wrote *Carry Them Back From Old Virginity* must be an extraordinary man. It was a daring work, boldly conceived, brilliantly executed. Was it banned in America?"

"Only in Boston, but that helped the sales. Forget about me. Tell me about yourself."

She laughed and marched back to the desk. From a rear view, her rump did not suffer by comparison. The ring motif was merely trebled in size. Nay, quadrupled.

"*Mais non,* my dear colleague. First you will tell me why you have chosen this time to honor us with your presence."

"Oh, that little thing."

"Yes, that. I must know. You see, I have a new program coming on the calendar and if you will be here long enough, perhaps I too can learn something about Sex from the great Professor Damon."

"I see." I stared at the nipples of her gorgeous artillery. "Well, frankly, Madame de Jussac, I'm in Paris as an advisor to one of the delegations for the peace talks. I can't tell you who really. You understand. Security and all that. Being here, a stone's throw from this famous institution, I thought I'd take a look-see. Even professors learn things as they go along. I have never stopped studying, you know."

Her eyes studied me. Her mouth, very wide and finely lipped, ran over a pink tongue.

"But what would you, a sexologist, have to contribute to something as political as a peace conference?"

"Ah, that's our secret, you see. But you surely do understand that there can be no harmony among nations if there is no harmony in the sex patterns and cultures of those nations."

"Yes, that's true." Her eyes suddenly shone. "But, certainly! Love is the answer, as always."

"Sure. We get Ho Chi Minh tattooed properly and he wouldn't waste his time running around ruining things. Ten to one he hasn't had his ashes hauled properly in years and that's what's bothering him."

"You must be right. There is no other explanation for so much killing, so much cruelty. I wish a man like you were the leader of a country. What a difference your regime would make!"

"My regime is your regime," I said gallantly, still working on those breasts. "Now tell me about Madame de Jussac. First name first."

She laughed and sat down behind the desk. She gave me a break and folded her arms across her chest. Or rather she didn't give me a break.

"Lilly is my name." Her voice was crisp and business-like. The major in her. "I am a native of Paris. Montmartre in '45. Yes, the war baby you might say. I never knew my father, perhaps he was one of your lovable G.I. Joes. I really do not care. My mother was killed in Paris during a bit of street fighting. The riots of '49. Since then, I did little except work, go to school. I graduated with honors in the social sciences and eventually all that led me here. I found that knowledge about sex and the human body and heart was all that interested me. Well, that is all there is to it. A dull story, I should think."

"Not dull. Just incomplete. You left out the juicy parts, Madame. Did you not?"

A shadow passed across her face. She almost sighed.

"Yes, I was married. Unfortunately, because of my lack of experience and knowledge, I chose a man who was more of a woman than I was. A sweet creature, all butter and chocolate. In fact, as homosexual as a—" She groped for a simile or adjective.

"Gay as a green goose?"

"*Merci*. As gay as that. In time, we divorced. He hung himself a year later with the cummerbund of his lover, a fat, disgusting munitions maker who since has gone to his own reward. Men!" She shook her head sadly, then suddenly snapped out of it. Her eyes, which I now saw were green, sparkled. "*Alors*. That is the story of one Lilly de Jussac. We will speak no more of it. Now, what can I do to make your visit here pleasant?"

"You could take off the rest of your clothes."

She didn't even blush. I realized then that she couldn't. Her real secret had crept out during some of her sad tale.

"Be serious. Surely, you would like to see the building. The classrooms. You could speak with the students. That's it, of course. Would you care to address the ladies in a series of lectures? They are excellent students, easily adaptable and would amaze you with their resourcefulness."

"Sure. I'll talk to them. I'll be in Paris indefinitely. Line me up a few engagements and I'm your man."

"You're a strange man. You accept so readily."

"I have to. The race is to the swift; we're only going to be on this earth a short time; eat, drink and be merry—and all that jazz. What else is there?"

"Indeed." She looked thoughtful and sat back in the chair. Her arms dropped and the Eastern and Western Hemispheres rose into the sunlight. "What else is there?"

"Name something. I'm game."

Her face broke into a smile. "I have it. Would you like to witness the latest point in our program? You realize we teach all forms of sexual union here. The Sexual, Homosexual, Heterosexual, Animal Farm, the Asexual,

Voyeurism, Frotteurism—all of those must be taught for a greater understanding of the extent and depth of the sexual in man and woman. Do you agree?"

"But why Frotteurism? That's a new one on me."

"To thrill those poor souls who get their excitation by rubbing against people. They do little else. Like in the theatres, the Metro—surely you have them in America?"

"In droves. On the IRT, the BMT, any crowded train."

"You see? So—let me show you how our ladies are being taught the niceties and, er, unniceties of lesbian contact. We don't have to leave the office. You have only to give me the word."

"You got it. Home, Lilly."

She frowned, shrugged her shoulders and reached for the French phone. She murmured something into it, hung up again and stood up. She stretched her lithe body and stalked to the big monster bed left over from a historical movie. She wasn't wearing any shoes. The better to feel the leopard skin rug with, I supposed.

She couldn't kid me much longer. All her actions and reactions were those of the dyed-in-the-wool Lesbian. I can tell. If I can't tell, I've been stealing money for years. Madame Lilly had been born a bastard, never knew her parents, married a tweety-bird and never came down off the tree. So she had taken the easy way out. No man was going to top her and do what had been done to her mother. You could see it all so clear. The only question was, was it too late to save her? Was she too old to change her spots? She was Lesbo by right of vengeance. She was unique, by right of—*what?*

The door opened about five minutes later and in trooped Mady Morrow. I might have known. Mady was wild-eyed, breathing hard and very eager. She was marching smartly to the desk and saluting. Tie that, will you?

Madame Lesbo frowned.

"What are you doing here? I wanted Viviane."

Mady kept a straight face. "Poor girl took sick with a dizzy spell right out in the corridor. So I came instead. Is that all right, Madame?"

Lilly fumed and looked at me.

"Damn fine with me," I said, trying to be agreeable. "I
40

like watching this one. She is so round and firm and fully packed."

The Madame shrugged. "Morrow is well and good but I wanted to show you Viviane. She is one of those soft, sweet, fragile creatures. The Lesbian motif suits her to the nth. Morrow here is rather a buxom wench. A bull, if you will."

"Then you be the cow," I suggested.

That one hit a nerve. She stiffened and Mady Morrow was trying to keep a straight face.

"Very well. If you insist. But *only* on choice of female. I do not play a cow well. I instruct my ladies in how to perform as love slaves. Get on the bed, Morrow."

"Yes, Madame."

Mady twitched over to the bed. She winked at me as she went by, fooling nobody. She had outsmarted the Madame, filled in for the missing Viviane and obviously just wanted me to see her in her feminine glory so I could drool a little wondering about our scheduled rendezvous. She was already climbing out of the middie blouse and stepping from the leather mini-skirt. She wore nothing under these items, either. What a school. The numberless enrollees probably didn't have a silk handkerchief between them.

Before the show got on the bed, I had a question for Madame Lilly de Jussac, whose oddities were apparently no secret to her girls.

"What's with the major bars? Were you in the Army?"

Mady Morrow had opted for turning the counterpane down and rolling back the blankets to the foot of the bed. All of her immense proportions bobbled, bubbled and ringadingdinged as she did so. She kept winking at me and stuck her tongue out. What a carnal babe she was. Completely uninhibited. With all the meat in Chicago.

Lilly paused, her mini-skirt dangling from her right hand. I tried not to gape. The incredible body, tapering, creamy, magnificent, was adorned with a Venus mound of red flaming glory. That was one thing I was going to have to find out for myself. Nobody is red down there. Not that red.

"Yes, I was a major. In the French Secret Service, some several years ago. I retain the rank only because it is a touch of masculinity and allows for the ladies to respect my rank and place as their head. Their Madame, as it were."

"Shrewd move, psychologically speaking."

"Yes, I rather thought so. Now if you will make yourself comfortable in that chair and watch, you will see how much Morrow and the other ladies of the *Académie Sexualité* have learned in so very short a time. I promise you will not be bored."

"Mind if I take notes?"

"By all means."

"Then, set to, ladies. I'm all eyes."

Madame Lilly de Jussac chuckled. It was a rich, venomous laugh that actually sent cold chills up and down my spine. It had cruelty and cold-bloodedness written all over it. The way Jack the Ripper might have laughed while he was cutting up in Whitehall.

"In a very little while, Monsieur Rod, I suspect"—and here she lay back on the bed, spread-eagling her splendid body—"that you will not be able to make that claim so easily. Indeed, you may very well be *all something else.*"

"Show me," I challenged.

"I shall. Mady"—her voice fell to a whisper—"kiss me, please. The way I showed you in the assembly hall."

"Ooolalala!" Mady Morrow chortled in her ungovernable, spirited way. "Lie back, Madame, and I'll do you to perfection!"

Madame Lilly de Jussac closed her eyes. Her lips moved. Barely in a whisper.

"Idiot," she said, without malice. "You mouth stupid things. You must be tender, sweet, loving and kind. You must draw from me all forms of desire and want and need so that I will respond. Now, do as I say. Begin at the beginning. Way down at my toes. The soles of my feet . . . *ahhhhh* . . . yes, yes . . . now slowly . . . do not rush . . . we must show Professor Damon so many things . . . must we not?"

The woman's voice was magic. Sheer magic.

It had to be. For Mady Morrow shut up and got going. Moving with slow, incredible grace. I watched, fascinated. I had underestimated the female head of the *Académie Sexualité.* My superior attitude about her lesbianism, however

42

true it was, could not justify what was happening before my eyes.

Or excuse what was happening to me, quick like a bunny.

I had lost all my ballast and the balloon was beginning to soar. Up, up and away!

Voyeurism, frotteurism—you name it. I don't care what the hell you call it. The indisputable fact of the matter and the awful unvarnished truth was, that watching that amazing redhead tangle with that buxom blonde on that big monster of a bed, earned for me one of the throbbingest erections I have had in my life.

It Sequoia'd from my thighs, straining for the ceiling of the room, wanting to be free, yearning to swing from its moorings. Man, I was hard.

And Madame Lilly had worked the miracle all with her magic little Lesbian act. She must have been a straight-A student.

Mesmerized, I watched the two loving figures on the bed.

It was *The Kiss* triumphant; Rodin sculpture gone hogwild. The Madame was a naughty lady. A very naughty lady, indeed. Naughty but oh, you Kid!

Madame Lilly de Jussac.

The one, the only, the original Frenchy.

Mady Morrow was no slouch either.

Between the two of them, they wrote a brand-new chapter of French history. The kind they can never teach at institutions of academic learning in America.

This was real *extra*-curricular activity!

43

CHAPTER FOUR

As *Soixante-Neuf* goes, it was in a class by itself. The redhead was one of Nature's wonders and the blonde was about a lap behind in the looks and deportment league. I got real uncomfortable on the chair, my eyes glued to the action. It was like having your own stag movie. The Madame's private office had become a smoker.

The girls were blazing away on the big bed. Mady had gone down in flames of desire, her great dexterous tongue licking into the fiery foliage that formed the convex of the de Jussac Venus mound. For a long moment, there was nothing but two sets of shapely thighs kicking and threshing, nothing but a revolving kaleidoscope of superb posterior and unforgettable breast structure. The blonde head blossomed at the core of the game. Madame de Jussac's red hair fluttered in the breeze. But she contributed more than a passive lovely body to the proceedings. The woman was a past mistress in the weaving of daisy chains. She'd been down that road before.

It was all too apparent.

Skillfully she had jounced her lithe body, working her long legs masterfully. She had hooked her tapering, slender fingers beneath Mady Morrow's armpits and wilfully, almost tenderly, thrust the bouffant head into her core. Mady came without a whimper, adding all of her weight as she put her pink tongue into it. There was a heady, intoxicating interval of syrupy noises, punctuated by long, heartfelt sighs and murmurs of endearment. Mady had abandoned her coarse Americanisms, but mysteriously, she had forgotten her rotten French accent too.

"Madame, Madame, Madame," she whispered fervently, an awestruck schoolgirl.

"Mady, Mady, Mady," the Madame replied, in a voice like the wind stealing over a haunted house.

"*Ai, yi, yi,*" I said to myself, straining on the chair. There was no holding the new strength within me. I was lifted off the chair, wanting to run wild. But I held back. There was more to see and learn.

44

The passionate human pretzel on the bed reversed with a startling lack of confusion. With remarkable ease, the twin beauties rotated and the blonde head replaced the red one. Or vice versa. Mady must have been good, to judge by the Madame's glazed sleepy-lidded look and utter smoothness of damp body. A fine sheen of lover's dew tinted her superb flesh. But Mady must have been an amateur. To judge by what came next.

Once during my impressionable youth, I watched a Greenwich Village daisy chain composed of three men and three women. The pecking order was changeable and far from completely heterosexual but what Madame de Jussac now did to Lilly reminded me of that time. The buxom blonde didn't have to wait to die to go to heaven. She was making the Pearly Gates in five seconds flat.

The Madame plunged her exquisite face, tongue first, into Mady's valley of decision. After that, the whole room exploded with a rapid-fire medley of grunts, groans, moans and veritable meows of feminine exaltation. Mady took off. In her delirium, she pawed feebly at the counterpane, she mashed the Madame's head, she kicked a hole into the ozone of the room. And then, after I don't know how long, there was one long loving yell and the bodies on the bed stopped moving. A cloud of invisible steam might have risen about the brocaded bed. Why not? A sexual Hydrogen bomb had certainly just exploded.

In a pool of my own sweat, I watched on.

The Madame and Mady lay subdued, crumpled, like scatter rugs flung across the bed. Their lovely mounds of womanhood, in all three areas, rippled and rose and fell with their hoarse breathing. I got hold of myself, lifted gingerly from my chair and went over to the bed.

"Time?" I laughed. "I thought you girls were real troupers. Tsk, tsk."

The Madam's low laugh emanated from the fleshpile.

"Ah, you jest. But tell me—was it not a delight to watch? You see how well Mady learns her lessons?"

"Private tutoring?" I suggested.

She didn't reply, only laughing. That cruel, vicious laugh that said so clearly what she was.

I unzipped my fly. The horse sprang from the barn. The metallic noise and the *whish* of passage of arms, made the

45

Madame bolt upright in bed. Her eyes saw me. Saw *it* and her nostrils flared and the red hair bristled and her green eyes shot hatred.

"Put that away or you will never enter this *Académie* again, my dear Monsieur Rod."

"Aw, c'mon. Have a heart. You had yours. What about mine? I could add years to your life with some of my own instruction."

"That is not necessary," she said icily and put her feet on the floor on the far side of the bed. Mady hadn't moved. The Madame's incredibly lovely back was to me. I fumed for a moment, and then forgot my discomfort. Mady's warm hand had stolen across the coverlet and vised me where it felt good. I stood there and sighed. It wasn't what I wanted but Mady's fingers were stroking me, then working up and down. It felt marvelous all the same. I looked down at her. Her eyes were still closed, her body a sprawl of sated womankind but her busy little fingers never let up. I had to stop her though. I was so prepared at that point, I could have shot the Madame right between the shoulder blades and pinned her to the other wall of the room. Like an oil canvas.

"Wouldn't you like to see me in action, Madame?"

"I'm afraid not. This is a woman's *académie*—not a stud farm. We don't want to cause chaos here, do we?" She had turned, standing up, wriggling into the leather mini-skirt. She had moved too fast. So that she saw Mady's hand working its points. For a moment, she trembled at the sight of a man. Her torso quivered and she sucked her breath in. But it passed and she was her own sweet Lesbian self again.

"Morrow!" Her voice was a whip. "Stop that!"

"Aw, Madame—" Mady's answer was a beg of sound.

"Stop it, I said. At once, do you hear?"

"Gee, whiz—can't a girl have any fun?"

"Morrow!"

"Okay, okay. I heard you."

The hot hand left me. I shrugged, gathered up the slack and repacked my pants. I managed a grin I didn't feel.

"*Regardez!*" I said. "Now you see it, now you don't."

Mady sat up, stretching her fleshy arms. She rubbed herself under the armpits. Her full chest load flared. But

46

her eyes were two happy pools. She'd gotten her jollies, but good.

"Okay, Madame? Can I go now?"

"Yes, return to your desk. Professor Damon will be back. I have persuaded him to give you ladies the benefits of some of his knowledge. Vocally, that is. A symposium is to be arranged."

"Gee, that's swell! Wait'll I tell the girls." She scrambled off the bed and redressed. From my chair, I looked at the Madame. The mad marry scene of only minutes ago could have happened to two other women. She was calm, cool and collected behind her desk again. She clapped her hands and Mady Morrow, so help me, practically curtsied and backed out of the room. But her glowing eyes reminded me to look her up first chance I got. The very first chance.

When the door had closed, Madame de Jussac got back to me.

"Well, Monsieur Rod?" She wasn't even breathing hard.

"What do you want me to say?" I growled. *"Vive la France?"*

"I want you to admit that this sort of instruction does show my ladies how to completely enjoy their femininity. Their vital essence, their feminine mystique, as it were."

"Sure. But what about the other side of the bed? Or are fifty million Frenchmen really wrong?"

Her eyes glittered. "That part is their own business. Here at the *Académie* we discuss it, show movies and even allow for visual aid courses, but since no man is allowed within the study walls—" Her topless body shrugged and the hemispheres barely collided. "The point is, we teach desire and the art of manipulation. As well as our libraries and records, which contain so many of your own works, by the way."

"I'm touched." There wasn't anything else I was going to ask her. She wasn't going to deliver the bacon and she hadn't once mentioned the murder of Danielle Lebeau. I decided to get my information on that matter elsewhere. "Well, I'm buzzing off. I'm staying at the Hotel *Fourchette*. When you get your schedule, set me up. I should be in Paris for a while. Okay?"

"Yes, thank you." She watched me reach the door

47

without getting up from the desk. I wondered about that until she said, "Tell me, Monsieur Rod. As penises go, you must be quite an over-sized male. Yes?"

"I'm real gone, Madame Lilly."

"Tres bien. You wouldn't care to tell me exactly how, ah, long you are?"

"Let's just say I'm smaller than a breadbox but bigger than a Nathan's special."

"Nathan's? What is that?"

"Coney Island in America. He sells hot dogs. Great big things. There's one that——"

"I see. I think I understand."

"I wish you did," I said sadly. *"Au revoir,* Lilly. We will meet again."

"A bientot," she purred. So I left her, letting her think it was Game and she had taken all the tricks. The knotty-pine steel door closed behind me and I had left the half-world of the heady pussycat of the *Académie Sexualité.*

A bee in toe—I'd like to have put a bee in her bonnet. All the way up until it stung her into drooling insanity. Clever broads irritate the hell out of me sometimes. They just aren't natural.

The corridor looked like clear-sailing. Not a streamlined student in sight. I headed down the hall, passing a lot more steel doors and entrances and exits. I was thinking about a lot of things but I'm no real detective. My mind was on Sex. Mady Morrow, in particular. Damn her being stuck at the Registration Desk—just my lousy luck.

ESP gets better all the time. And perhaps it is merely that minds that run along libidinous channels simply have to meet. It's like two testicles that beat as one.

I'd just about reached the bend in the hall that branched out into the big lobby when a door on my left whipped open, two soft hands reached out and practically swept me off my feet. I went without a whimper. I followed flashing eyes, an open red mouth and a quivering pale blur of female body. Speak of the Angel!

Mady Morrow was way ahead of me.

A lock clicked, a dim light flicked on and I found myself in the broom closet. There was a mop, a pail, boxes of all kinds of detergents and rows of shelves that held nothing but laundry soap, brillo pads and that soapy smell

48

that clears out the nostrils in no time at all. But there was also Mady Morrow, cramming me up against the wall, roving her hands all over me, licking hungrily at my face. I let her. There wasn't much room but you don't need a bed to tango. Not always. Close confines can be enough.

"You meanie," she whispered hungrily. "Did you think you were going without seeing me—?"

"You'll never believe it," I said, grabbing handfuls of her and letting them warm my fingers. She felt big and soft and marshmallowy and I was in a toasting mood. She sighed as her fingers undid my trousers and the family jewels glittered in the gloom. "I wanted you back there with Madame."

"Her?" Mady snorted. It was like a fine young filly stamping in a stall. "Tongues are okay but they'll never replace *this*. Jeezis, Professor, is that really all you?"

"Find out for yourself."

"Golly!" she lowered herself to her knees, clasping her hands around my fanny. Her mouth found me. Thrills shot up and down my spine. I leaned against the door for leverage and pushed. She gulped hungrily, her lips racing. When her nails dug into my skin, I lifted her up and set her down on it. She squealed with pleasure, riding it, hooking her ample thighs around my waist. Her soft blind spot dampened, vising me tightly until some spasmodic jerks and pushes and rhythm from my end made her flood me.

"Ohhhhh," she moaned. "Jeezis, Rod—"

"What's the matter?"

"I came—here—to study and mind my P's and Q's but it's so *harrrrrd* to be good!"

"It's gotta be hard to be good and who says you're being bad?"

"The Madame—she—*oh, do that again*—yes, yes— she says we have to learn all about our bodies but she won't let any men help us in the classroom work—*stick me,* baby—oh, stop—*don't stop!*"

I didn't. I was all stored up, the scene on the bed having made me infernally savage and strong. I leaned Mady against her wall without having to move more than a yard of space. Between the brooms and the detergents, I had her boxed up solid. She had the goods too. So all she did

49

was benefit by my enforced diet. I was ravenously hungry.

We didn't talk for the next twenty minutes.

Not until I had taken her standing up, sideways, backways and up and down. For a really big young girl, she was deft and graceful. Her muscles and coordination were as good as any highly trained athlete. Finally, for an encore and a finishing stroke, I salvaged Yankowski's favorite position, as he had outlined in his memorable keystone work, *Vertical Or Horizontal, The Man As Aggressor*. The old Polish great was convinced that the male must inevitably assume the role of attack, piercing the core of the apple, stabbing the circle, meeting the V, keying the lock. Or, splitting the atom, to coin a phrase.

So Yankowski's perfect thrust was: come in at a forty-five degree angle and go about as far as you can go. Yankowski erred in one important particular. He never specified in which position the female of the species should, or must be. But that really didn't matter. At forty-five degrees, it is always every man for himself, isn't it? And woman.

Mady Morrow was leaning back into the gloom of the closet but she was wide open and waiting and willing. I got some jumping room, targeted in on her and plunged. After that, we dissolved into a tangle of fused, smoking flesh on the floor. It was a union of Titans. Mady was good. I told her so as we huddled, cheek to cheek, among the mops and brooms. Or whatever that closet held.

"Geezis," she muttered. "Coming from you—"

"I mean it. You're wasting your time and money in this joint. Anybody else use this closet?"

"Only me. I got the key. Rest of these chicks are all afraid of Madame. Isn't she a pip?"

"A living doll. But a waste of womanpower. Her pipes will get rusty without a real plumber."

"Hell with her." Mady nuzzled her mouth against my pectorales major and minor. She'd managed in her own primitive way to get some of the clothes off me. "Why don't we get married?"

"We can't. I'm promised to a million others."

"I believe it," she sighed. "It would be a shame to put a ball and chain on that beast."

50

I bit her ear. "Forget us for a while. Would you answer me a few questions?"

"Anything!"

"Good girl. Did you know Danielle Lebeau?"

It was amazing. Mady Morrow suddenly started sobbing. I had my hands full comforting her. The big bountiful body shivered with sorrow.

"Hey, what's all this?"

"Sorry," She sniffled. "Dany was such a swell chick. A real gal. Brains too. It was so stupid her running around with that fat old Corbeau character. He couldn't even get it up, you know. Dany told me—said all he ever wanted was to be seen with her—to take her out, show her a good time. Like her old man, really——"

"Whoa, horsey. A little slower. You *knew* Danielle Lebeau, then?"

"Sure. Her room was on the same floor as mine. We talked a lot together. About sex, the Academy—I really liked her. You would have flipped for her, Rod. She was a living doll. Looked a lot like Hedy Lamarr used to."

"Then it was a waste. This Dany ever talk about anything else?"

"No. You kidding? In this place, it's nothing but sex. That's what we're here for, isn't it? Everybody wants to forget where they came from, who they were. Didn't you ever go to college?"

I laughed. "Thought you knew all about me? I matriculated at Denver and won my reputation. And my career. By the way, what did you do to Viviane and why aren't you on the desk?"

"Money talks, Handsome. I slipped Viviane ten bucks to let me fill in for her with Madame. Viviane didn't mind. The Madame's been biting too much lately. Viviane's spelling me at the desk right now."

"Hussy." I pinched her right breast. She giggled happily. Then, soberly, she had a last comment upon Danielle Lebeau.

"Poor Dany. Why would anybody stick a knife in her?"

"Could be a sex crime. From what I hear she was prim and virginal. Was she? She could have gotten herself killed holding out."

"Dany? She was a sweetheart, I told you. Face like an angel."

"Speaking of faces, where could I get a picture of her? I'd like to see what she looked like."

Mady Morrow was silent for a long moment.

"Damn," she said. "Talk about coincidences. Wait'll I turn on the light. This'll kill you."

"Then I don't want to see it."

"No, no. It's peculiar, that's all. Dany took a photo once for a magazine and I stuck it on the door of this damn closet because we couldn't put it in the dorm or in our rooms. Madame would have had a fit. And she'd never come in here, naturally. So I tacked it up on this door—wait—*there*!" She had turned on a dangling bulb. Light, pale and yellow, flickered feebly. But I could see what she meant. On the roomside of the door was an incredibly large, calendar size magazine-style photo of Danielle Lebeau. I almost whistled. Not even *Playboy's* centerfold had ever matched the daring nudity of this shot. Hugh Hefner would have had lawsuits galore.

Mademoiselle Lebeau was a long-legged brunette of exceedingly elfin face and fantastic endowments. In the shot, she was standing with her back to a leopard-skin wall motif with her arms held out and her body poised and ready. The ruddy triangle was hidden only by a tasseled bell-pull which she had wrapped around her loins with all the come-on of the old-time burlesque runways. But you could see it all.

Mady Morrow was right. The face was Lamarr lovely, the dark hair framing perfection. Danielle Lebeau's eyes held enchantment and seduction. So professional looking that it was hard to credit the virginal tales told about her. And what sort of girl poses like that for national survey?

I looked more closely.

The photo had been on page forty-seven of a magazine called *Paris Burning* and was datelined on the bottom. The date was only two months ago. I peered further. On the upper corner of the page, left hand, someone had scrawled an address with a blue pen.

"What's that?"

"Oh, where her mother lives. Mrs. Lebeau. I scribbled it on—look, you can have the picture if you want it. Doesn't

52

seem right to leave it hanging there now that Dany's dead."

"Thanks. I'll take it. Before we leave this closet. How come the police didn't confiscate that? They're investigating her murder, aren't they?"

Mady shrugged and her breasts spilled out at me again. I patted them affectionately. She was proving a gold mine in many ways.

"Madame swings a lot of weight with the government. She let them case Dany's room and talk to her friends, but they couldn't step foot in any other part of the Academy. Listen, I wrote Dany's address down because I cut the picture out and I wanted to know if she wanted her mother to see it. But Dany didn't—she was ashamed of that photo but the rest of the girls thought it was groovy."

"What was her excuse for posing for it then?"

"She never told me. But I got the impression that it was kind of forced on her, you know what I mean? She wouldn't talk about it at all but it embarrassed the hell out of her."

"Thanks, Mady. You've been a big help."

"You can show your appreciation better than that." She reached down again and raised the flag. I nodded, happy with her. She was fun to ball, a fount of information and just plain marvelous. Groovy, like she had said.

"Okay. Time for one more. For the road."

"The road?" She pouted. "You're never going to say goodbye to me, Roddy. I want you again and again and again. All the time you stay in Paris. Mister, I'm going to have to talk myself out of not following you halfway around the world."

"You're sweet, you know that." I kissed the tips of her breasts to prove how sweet she was. "Mmmmmmmmm."

She settled back, closing her eyes, letting me, while her busy thighs widened to permit me to enter customs again. I slipped through without any effort at all. She was lubed to the nth degree now and it was like having it throw its arms around you. I was more than welcome in that neck of the woods.

"Rod, baby . . ."

"Yes, doll?"

"What was that guy's name? The scientist who invented that last move you showed me?"

53

"You mean Yankowski?"

"Yeah. Yankowski . . . Rod . . . ?"

"I," I said, "am not going anywhere."

"Yank me again."

Sex. It's marvelous. Truly marvelous. In the midst of life, when you are involved with death, there just isn't any other way to go. It doesn't solve anything, of course, and it certainly doesn't bring anybody back to life, but oh, my friends, and oh, my foes, and oh, oh, my girls, nothing in the world is quite like it. The poultice of passion is good for all wounds. Including the incurable wound.

For the female wound, there is nothing like a male poultice applied with tender loving care.

Dealey, on his last legs at seventy-three and in failing health, given only a month to live by the family physician, staffed his baronial hall in Manchester with the naked chorus of a famous underground West End musical and cavorted like the Petronius of old before his heart finally gave out. The grand old man of British sexology accounted for one half of the female chorus (some twenty-ones dames in all) before he folded up like an umbrella. As he died, he shouted, *"By George, I've got it!"* Sad to relate, no one ever found out exactly what he meant or might have discovered at seventy-three. The story is perhaps apocryphal but it is legendary in sexology circles. It never made the papers, naturally, because Dealey has three M.P. relatives in government.

But he went the way we all secretly want to. Riding high, on the rise and in the full splendor of his powers. A fitting finish for a man who lived for love—or at least sex.

Yankowski, De Grand, Nokama of Japan, Damon—all of us—yearn for that finest hour. In the end, we'll all go down swinging. It's the only way to live if you are to die right.

Mady Morrow was panting like a steam engine. Yankowski's method had driven her to the wall. She was shuddering like a tree in a high wind. I was pruning her for all I was worth.

"Dammit, Damon—don't you ever stop!"

"I, dear lady, do not every stop anything I start."

"That's good," she gurgled, "kinda like we understand each other. As one American to another."

54

"Oui."

"Wee, my foot. If you were any bigger I'd be standing out in the hall. Oh, Roddy, baby. . . ."

She certainly did like Yankowski's method, with Damon Body English, of course. Somehow, we had managed to become one, indelibly. My pores could have been imprinted all over her. We were balled up in one torchy, scalding knot of male and female harmony. Not even the long, low thwacking noises that accompanied our hectic union could have been heard in the hallway beyond the broom closet. There was something so incredibly soft and sweet and soaring about Mady. For all her rough and tumble, sock-me-and-rock-me overtures of aggressiveness, she was all sweet and syrupy surrender at the proper times. But her surrenders were no Waterloos. Not by a jugful. She couldn't lose for winning. Whatever we did together, she came away a richer more fulfilled woman. She knew it all the way and in the knowing lay her great secret of survival. The girl was terrific.

"Wait a mo, Rod . . . just hold it . . ."

She had cranked her pelvic cage around so that she was hitting me from a weirdly wonderful angle of her own. In the darkness, I couldn't be sure just where she was.

"Like that?" I asked.

"Yeah, yeah," she chortled huskily. "Now—get going that way and don't you ever stop!"

It wasn't a question so I didn't answer it.

"Ohhh!"

"Roger," I said.

"Ooooo!"

"Check," I agreed.

"Ahhhhh!"

"You can say that again."

She did. All three versions of the testimonial to my priapic power.

At last she sagged against me and the clocks had run down. The little dark closet was a bower of love. We had really mopped up.

"Oh, that smarts," she muttered.

"Yes. But it's the smartest thing in all this cockeyed world."

55

"You," she giggled. "What a man. Always talking about sex."

Of course, she was right. But in my own curious way, I had exorcized the painful ghost of a lovely French girl, Walrus-moustache's cynical face, and the hovering dark clouds that threatened the peace talks in Paris.

Rod Damon's the name, Sex is my game.

Half an hour later I had escaped from the broom closet, and Mady Morrow had gone back up to her room by a back staircase to take a long hot shower. I had made more than sexual progress. I had learned that the *Académie Sexualité* was being run by one notorious Lesbian and I had a good clear photo of the murdered Lebeau chick and the address where she had lived. It was neatly folded in my coat pocket. Also I had to wonder why the Madame hadn't cared to mention the tragic end of one of her brightest students, to judge by the thesis called *Sex and Concentration*. You see, I am sort of an agent after all. I'd gotten into the snooping habit, thanks to past experience and Walrus-moustache and the Thaddeus X. Coxe Foundation.

I passed the Resistration Desk on the way out. A quiet, madonna-like brunette beauty was quietly reading the copy of *Candy*. She looked about eighteen but the equipment more than matched the lusty girl shown on the paperback cover. I kept on moving but my shadow or aura or clicking heels made the girl look up. Large dark eyes swept over me. The middie blouse was jam-packed with goodies and a flash of crossed legs under the leather mini-skirt would make a sex fiend out of a lay minister. I wasn't surprised that this might be Madame Lilly de Jussac's speed. The girl was soft, creamy, a horde of curves and dimples. Not a lusty, busty extrovert like Mady Morrow.

"Come back, Professor Damon," she called out in a low sweet voice.

"Viviane, of course."

"*Oui, monsieur.*"

"*Oui, oui*, indeed. Catch you the next time around. And don't believe a word of that book. It's strictly for laughs and sex is no laughing matter."

Her wide eyes smiled. I had a last glimpse of her, white teeth, knockers and all.

"It is too absurd," she agreed. "Still it has its points. But

56

I defer to your superior estimate. When you come again, ask for Viviane Fresnay. Room three-two-nine."

With a cheery *au revoir*, I exited from the *Academié Sexualité* without further incident. Most of the sleepwalking lovelies in mini-skirts had disappeared, buried in the classrooms of that august edifice. It was quite a temple of learning. Yearning, that is. When a woman cracks a book to find out all about me, the damage has already been done. They've got their bets in, you could say.

The bleak boulevard beyond the quadrangle was crawling with French taxicabs. I hailed one, climbed in and gave the moustachioed driver the address of Mrs. Lebeau. Mrs. Brigitte Lebeau. There was no way of getting around it. The search was on and I had to do the rest of my job.

I had to see the mother about the daughter.

The cabbie, a lipburner almost out of sight under his scrubby moustache, cranked his meter flag down and droned off toward the Montmartre section. The Eiffel Tower was spiring like a ready phallus in the distance, ready to screw the skies.

It was an omen.

Little did I know there was going to be another hot time in the old town tonight.

Paris wasn't only burning—it was going down in flames.

CHAPTER FIVE

Danielle Lebeau's mother lived on one of those blocks that's maybe only a hundred and fifty feet long, rising like a hill, and dotted with bistros, cafes and striped canopy like something from a Hollywood musical of the fantastic Forties. Number Ten was about four stories high, a walk-up and an iron railing corkscrewed. Madame Lebeau's was on the third floor back with a gloomy wreath still cluttering the door. Danielle's mother had obviously been hit hard, considering the fact that the tragedy was old news.

I tapped lightly on the door, trying not to hold my nose. The hallway, narrow and dimly lit, reeked of old cabbage cooking and empty beer cans. It was hard to imagine a doll like Danielle Lebeau coming from a background like this.

There was a pause and then a rattle of bolts and the door opened. For a moment, I was confused. As bad as the light was, the dame in the doorway didn't look like anybody's little gray-haired old lady.

"Yes, please?"

The woman looked only about twenty-five and would have given Brigitte Bardot a run for her bathtowel. This one was wrapped in a housecoat of silk all covered with yellow sunflower pattern and a belt that was carelessly looped so that the opening of the coat showed me at least two of the main glories of France. The woman was built like a brick wall and there was enough petulance in her red mouth and eyes to make me feel like a vacuum cleaner salesman. But also, it was obvious right off that this was Danielle Lebeau's older twin. It was the same kind of wide-eyed classic Paris face. Only the hair showed traces of becoming silver. Which were probably intentional.

"Yes, I am pleased, but I'm here on a sad errand. I want to talk about your sister to you."

"My sister?" The woman looked me up and down. "Another crazy American! I have but only one relative and she is dead—oh, my poor Danielle—" The woman

58

glared at me. "No more pictures—" She began to close the door. I inserted a quick shoe.

"*You* are Brigitte Lebeau? *Congratulations,* Madame. Unless I'm going blind you don't look a day over twenty-five."

Maybe she'd just lost a daughter but she'd gained an admirer and they still counted for plenty in her book. She stopped trying to force the door closed and looked my face over.

"Then you are not from the newspapers?"

"No."

"Or the police?"

"Never."

"Not being either of those despicable things, what is it you want then? This is not a *bordello* and there is one next door so perhaps you are mistaken—"

"Just give me a second—"

"Hah! If I give you that you could have my clothes off in a minute! I do not trust Americans. Particularly ones that look like you. My husband, may his testicles rot from mildew, ran off with an American chorus girl some fifteen years ago and I haven't seen him since. Curse that devil Gaspard. Well? Will you go or shall I scream that you have tried to rape me?"

I didn't waste any more time. I told her who I was, what I was and how I had been captivated by Danielle's thesis and flown directly to Paris to see her only to learn of her sad fate. As I talked, Madame Lebeau's face got sadder and sadder. But she believed me and the waterworks started all over again because I had brought back tender memories of her baby and pretty soon, she dragged me into her home, bolted the door and drew me toward a four-postered bed that cluttered the wall. That and some poor chairs and few prints of the Impressionists and a vase of dead flowers made the entire Lebeau domicile pass for what is laughingly called a home in some parts of the world. Danielle's mother was amazingly vibrant and unscarred by her thirty-seven years. She looked like twenty-five and acted like a frisky teenager. All the time she talked to me, she held both my hands in her lap, letting me feel the pulsing magnificence of her sturdy, womanly thighs. Her whim-whams were constantly threatening to flop out of the loose housecoat.

"So. You are Damon. *Le professeur*. How she admired your work! We talked about you so many times. I feel as if I know you well! Here—right here in this very room. On weekends she stayed with me. Then she would go back to her *Académie Sexualité*." Madame Lebeau made a disgusted face. "Why must the young things go to a school to learn how to be women?"

"It's a generation gap, Madame."

"Obscenity on their new ideas. Call me Brigitte. We have much in common. I see you too would like to avenge Danielle's death or you would not have come."

"Thank you. I *would* like to just know about her association with Gaston Corbeau. After all—" I looked around at the squalid surroundings. Brigitte Lebeau did not take offense. She was a woman of understanding as well as hot genes. Her thigh was rubbing my left hip away. Her heat would have defrosted a deep freeze unit.

"Even roses can bloom in a manure pile. But Corbeau is an old fool. My daughter was merely his friend. You will find nothing wrong in that. I doubt that it has anything to do with her murder." She placed her hand on her heart and closed her eyes. "Danielle, Danielle! Ah, the agony of loneliness. Dear professor, I am a lonely old woman."

"You aren't old and I'm here now."

"That is true. What can I do for you?" She opened her eyes and flung out her arms. Her full chest thrust out, trying to get past the folds of the housecoat. I wasn't hungry yet and I was still looking for information. I stood up and indicated the room with its lean-to and small kitchenette. At least, the place smelled fresh and flowery.

"I'd like to help, Brigitte. If Danielle had any things here—papers, clothes, books, keepsakes—could I see them? We might find something of interest."

She sighed and stood up, knowing now was perhaps not the time to play tiddlywinks. She gestured toward a corner of the room.

"Over there. The luggage. It is hers. The police claimed it on that day and returned it only yesterday. They seem to have found nothing. But feel free, *mon cher*. I need an aperitif. Join me?"

"A little, yes. This will only take me a minute."

60

While the youthful-looking mother poured a couple of jiggers of cognac for us, I got to work on the suitcase in the corner. It was alligator-leather, no stamps or markings. What was inside of it was important. Again, I was in for a surprise. Danielle Lebeau must have been two women. What do acknowledged sweet young things want with a storehouse of masochistic sex-cult trappings? As Madame Lebeau passed me a glass, I puzzled over the contents of the suitcase.

In the order I found them, they were riding whips, leather gauntlets with steel knuckles, leather boots, black leotards with an applique across the crotch that spelled out the words, HIT ME, BABY in French, several truncheon-sized dildoes and last but not least, a long black leather whip, tooled in gold which had emblazoned across its thorny hilt, the name *Danielle* in script lettering. I held it up and turned to her mother.

Brigitte Lebeau shrugged.

"I was as outraged as you when I first saw them. But Danielle told me it was part of her study assignments at the *Académie*."

"That's not possible. It's a love school not a hate school. If Madame de Jussac tried anything like that, it would have leaked out and she would have been kicked out. I was there this morning. Nobody gets beaten in that place. You never saw such healthy women in your life."

"So—what can I say?"

"What about this?" I showed her the personalized whip.

"A gift from an admirer, perhaps? Corbeau? Who can say? Young women meet all kinds nowadays, do they not?"

"Yea, verily." I was thinking about Madame de Jussac's Lesbo curriculum. Regretfully, I dropped the whip back into the suitcase and snapped the bag shut. Then my eye caught a framed portrait parked on a low china closet to one side of the lean-to. There was something very familiar about it. Danielle's mother saw me looking at it and laughed happily. A laugh of triumph and yeah, team!

"See for yourself," she urged. I did, picking up the photo in its gold-embossed frame. My memory meshed. The girl in the portrait was about thirteen years old, and in her elfin gamin beauty was all the vixenish, hoydenish,

61

sheer sexiness of a much older woman. There was a signed message on the photo. *To my Brigitte from her Emperor Nickie, who is her slave.*

"So that's who you are." I stared at Brigitte Lebeau. "You little hell-raiser. I should have recognized you."

She was pleased. Her chest swelled proudly.

"Now you know Fifi, eh? It is good. Yes I am she. Fifi Le Fleur, who at the age of thirteen seduced an emperor and won the admiration and disbelief of the world. Causing a king to forget his country, his wife, his children. That was a long time ago. Before I tired of courts and kings and came to Paris where I belonged. It was headline news all over the universe and I threw it all away for that fool of a Gaspard Lebeau. Curse the man and his infernally unforgettable wiggle! He drove me mad when we made love. Still—it was wonderful to be a courtesan. But I wanted babies—I wanted Danielle." She sniffled and flung herself into my arms.

"There, there, old girl—"

"I am not old!" She bumped her pelvic cage into my ball park. "Dare you ask me to prove it?"

"Only a figure of speech." I patted the firm, flexible muscles of her rump. "But first, we must investigate a bit more. Have we missed anything?"

"No—no, wait a moment—the book. That I did not give the *gendarmerie*. After all, if my dear daughter kept a diary, it was her affair. But it merely proved to be an address book. You wish it?"

"Most of course."

She padded to an escritoire that was really an end table and came back with a thick, black leather memo-type book. She was right, again. Nothing but French names, addresses and phone numbers. I riffled through it, trying to spot a familiar item. I was beginning to feel more and more like Ye Private Eyes Spade, Noon and Shayne.

"Is it of any use at all, Monsieur Rod?"

"I won't call you Madame if you don't call me Monsieur. No, I don't know."

"Those names mean nothing to me. Though I recognize the bordellos and pimps and gay places. I suppose Danielle would have told me they also were part of her studies. Ah, the children of today! How they abuse all our own past experience at living! How did they imagine we lived this long? By living in a vacuum? Bah!"

She vibrated with sudden anger. I dropped the book into my side pocket. I sipped the rest of my giddy cognac. It tasted real fine.

"Brigitte, I have an idea."

She had one too. The wrong one. Her eyes strayed to my belt buckle. She showed me her tongue. It flicked out like a snake tail.

"Yes?"

"I should like to begin a systematic search of these names. And places. You know—call up, go there, ask around. We could learn something."

"We?"

"Sure. If you are free tonight, I will be your escort. When I am done we will come back here for some more understanding of each other. Okay?"

She almost giggled but her hands came up to my face and she planted a resounding kiss on my mouth, adding another erotic bump for good measure. Poor Emperor Nickie. The bastard never had a chance.

"You do not think I am an old woman?"

"Who me? Don't be foolish."

"That is good. You are wise, dear Rod. For that I will show you my gratitude." Her hands came down from my face, roving for my waist. I grabbed her wrists.

"Later. Right now, pour yourself into your best bib and tucker and you'll show me Paris. From the first page in the book on. Now, hurry up and get dressed. I'll have some more cognac."

She whooped ecstatically and came out of her widow's weeds with a helluva yell. I got a flash of her *derriere* racing into the lean-to as she whipped off the housecoat. She had a rear end like a full moon over Miami. Or should I say, Montmartre?

I tried to like the cognac but I couldn't. So I had a glass of water instead. Again, progress. I had met Danielle Lebeau's mother, uncovered an address book the cops hadn't seen and maybe, just maybe, the answer to her murder was among all those names, addresses and places. The secret agent *schtick* was going great guns.

Brigitte Lebeau *née* Fifi Le Fleur was humming *The*

63

Marseillaise as she flung a million things around looking for some battle clothes to wear to the ball. I was loaded with Walrus-moustache's expense money so the sky was the limit.

Paris sky or not.

Danielle Lebeau's address book led us a merry chase. We began with the A's and worked our way through the alphabet. Madame Brigitte Lebeau was my girl guide. For the occasion, she provided herself with a feathered dress complete with spangles, which was about large enough to have covered a small owl. But the Madame was a wise old bird. She had the legs and breasts of a woman budding with life and she wanted to show off. I have to admit she looked like about nine million dollars. With her gleaming mini-dress, feathers and radiant face topped with the silver-streaked hair, she was a *Parisienne* knockout. I didn't mind at all. She could also hold her cognac, kept close to my side and did all the translating for me with waiters, doormen and maitre d's.

There were three *A* listings. The first one was a Theo Armand, who turned out to be a French bookie, currently in the Bastille for beating up a client. The second was a chick named Annie Allendon and it turned out that Annie didn't live there anymore. Her *concierge*, a fat, fierce beldame, demanded to know if we would pay the rent that was overdue. Mlle. Allendon seemed to be a two-dollar or fifty-franc whore. The third *A* was a homosexual named Charles Alain. He waved his wrists limply at us in a sidestreet bistro and claimed he hadn't seen Danielle Lebeau in months. He still couldn't believe she was dead, he said, crying. Madame Lebeau sniffed the air and dragged me away from him. *"These winged creatures!"* she rasped.

I didn't argue. I trusted Brigitte Lebeau's nose now.

The *B*'s were even less fruitful. Five names later— all working prositutes named Beloin, Barnet, Bubullay, Bousse and Borne, who just couldn't be found, according to their streetwalker pals—Madame Brigitte and I paused in the evening's occupation and decided to rest up.

I passed her the address book.

"Find a bistro under the *C*'s or *D*'s and let's park awhile.

64

We could run ourselves down this way."

She nodded, her eyes gleaming.

"You know, my dear Rod, you always refresh my memory."

"How so?"

"You saw the people we have already seen. What kind of people was my dear daughter interested in? Bookies, streetwalkers, *les pansies. Sacré bleu!* I remember now—there is a place she spoke of many times as a veritable laboratory for her studies. Under the *D*'s, I shall find the name I know it." she thumbed the pages. "Ah! And here it is—a pervert's paradise! *Les Deuces.* There all one's inhibitions are attended to. They service the normal and the abnormal. What you would call a 'mixed' bordello. Of a certainty, we will find a clue to Danielle's murderer there."

"Lays and gays, huh? Would you be safe in a place like that, I wonder?"

She favored me with a glare. "I have lived. I can take care of myself."

"All right. Where is it?"

Her smile was dirtier than the Seine.

"But three blocks from where we stand. Come, my American. You will really see the Paree underworld tonight."

I followed her, convinced more and more that there was something about Danielle Lebeau that did not meet the eye. My research takes me to a lot of out of the way places too, but it's different somehow when a vulnerable young chick, hardly of age, does it.

What *was* Danielle Lebeau really like?

Les Deuces was downstairs, under the cobbled streets of the city. No fooling. You took a manhole cover off the street, a doorman stuck his head out, Madame Lebeau slipped him a large franc note which I had supplied her with and down we went. When the manhole cover slipped shut over our heads, we descended a dark staircase that smelled of the sewers into another world. Underworld, my foot. It was a rathole with upholstered drapes and about twenty cubicles all roped off with velour trappings and carpets. The sewer stink disappeared once you got into the heart of the place. Incense was burning, along with about fifty gallons of fragrant perfume. The place looked like a cathouse, smelled like a cathouse and it was a cathouse. Even if it seemed to service the toms as well as the pussies.

Madame Brigitte Lebeau rubbed her hands together. I could see her breasts heaving. Her eyes had a supernatural glint.

"Ah, but this is a devil's joyhouse! Look about you."

I looked. Most of the cubicles had drawn drapes indicating a busy night but the floor of the strange place held enough half-naked whores to supply an army on furlough. There were brunettes, redheads, taffy blondes, purple heads and magenta heads, all lolling from hassocks and divans and ottomans. Nobody paid any attention to us. Some of the women were working. One particularly choice number with what seemed like a size 50 bust was languidly lying back against the wall, propped in a sitting position, while two long-haired young boys nibbled voraciously, one to each breast. The choice number couldn't have cared less. She was doing a crossword puzzle above their hungry heads. About three dames over, another weird scene was being enacted. There, two lively young things were pretzeled together, doing honor to the ancient honored custom of *soixante-neuf*. It was okay except for the fact that it was but another version of boys will be boys. It was easy though to tell who the customer was. One of the boys was a fat flabby little guy and the other was a bronzed giant who could have been wrestling with a kitten. That made me nervous. The bronzed queer was a brute and if he ever took notions to take off after me with his tools of the trade I wouldn't like the idea of fighting to save my ass.

I didn't like the place at all but Brigitte Lebeau was in a visitor's state of trance. In fact, she was in heat. Her painted fingernails were raking my arm.

"Look—if you're hurting," I said, "buy yourself a ride. We've got money to burn. But remember, we came here to learn what we could."

"No, no—I'm all right. It is just that the sight of so much carnality, so much freedom, turns my head. Ah, look at that little thing—is she not something?"

"That little thing" proved to be a long, lanky Chinese

66

girl with slanting eyes and slanting everything who was studiously making a fine meal out of the man standing before her. The poor customer had his eyes closed and was trying to remain standing up. It looked like a bet of some kind. Several of the whores lolling about were chanting and clapping their hands. Voices rose in a chorus of "*Un, deux, trois, quatre. . . .*" Before they reached ten, the poor guy went down to his knees and the lanky dragon lady sat back, wiping her gash of a mouth. She had taken one from A and one from B and finished off the customer. Again, what a way to go. She was licking her lips greedily.

"Who's in charge here?" I whispered to Brigitte. She shook her head, still enrapt with the scenes of glory all around. I could see it was useless. We had wasted our time. Half the joint was smoking pot or using giggle-sauce and I didn't expect to learn a damn thing down here. I'd seen it all too many times. Orgy without organization.

I took her arm. "Come on. Let's vamoose. Down here we won't get any straight answers. We couldn't't."

"But, not yet . . . please, *cherie* . . . I get out so little these days!" She made me feel like a killjoy of a parent.

"All right. Five minutes more. I hate to be a party-pooper but even I'm not safe in a flytrap like this."

The five minutes reprieve was a mistake. Brigitte Lebeau was so far gone that she lost her head. Oh, she didn't rip her clothes off and make like the natives. Not that. It's just that she spilled the beans. My beans. In a moment's deep indiscretion, she climbed atop a hassock and shouted for all that underworld to hear:

"Listen, everyone! Listen!"

She had a bellow like a foghorn in San Francisco bay. All eyes and ears, even the occupied ones, swung to stare at this bold, bawdy, magnificent dame crying for attention. I must admit, Birgitte looked marvelous. Like a French Lana Turner. The long-haired boys giggled.

"*Cheries!*" she exulted. "You have a famous guest this night! The great, the unparalleled, the unique, the man himself—Monsieur Rod Damon of America!"

That, as they say in police stations, did it.

The whores stopped lolling, the orgies slowed down, the atmosphere got electric, and pretty soon we were the center of a pinwheeling, excited mob of demimondaines,

67

fairies and eager perverts, dying for a look, firing a million questions. My fame, you see, is world-wide. Sex is important to many, many souls in this beknighted world of ours and hadn't I led the crusade for Truth and Experience down the dark ages of the Screwy Sixties?

What was worse, the bronze stud who had serviced the flabby little character came mincing over, muscles swinging, dong to the fore. His eyes were glowing and I didn't even have to guess what he wanted to do. He was at least eleven inches of swinging male meat and he was a cinch to want to match sizes. I was famous, he wasn't, except as a local marvel. You know the pitch. It's like all those guys who wanted to test Jack Dempsey's right cross in a barroom in the good old days.

Brigitte was in her glory. She cackled and crowed and pointed me out and I was swamped with clutching hands, mashing breasts and urging hips. Somebody even thrust a ballpen in my hands to make with the autograph. I was in a crush of bodies and it wasn't exciting. It was downright scary. We might not get out of that underground rathole with our skins intact. The dame with the 50's was goosing me.

I tried to smile, grabbing Brigitte Lebeau and moving her to the exitway. The bronze stud was circling the crowd, trying to cut us off. The prosties were hollering in French, gabbling like so many chickens and then it happened. One of them, maybe it was the long, lanky Chinese number, recognized Brigitte Lebeau. Remembered the story and history of Fifi Le Fleur. And the jig was up. All the way up. I was forgotten about, quick like a bunny, and the beautiful mother of the dead Danielle Lebeau was in for it. Two-dollar whores and fifty-franc prosties have their own curious envies and jealousies. When a woman of their own kind can price it as high as a king's throne, well, that's one dame they do admire—and like to put down. It's the only explanation for the mad balling scene that followed.

It was uncanny.

Almost by silent agreement, about five of the killing crowd closed in on me, pushing me to the far wall. I was trapped. The five were a mass of shouting, laughing, drugged women. But it wasn't my charm that made them

68

behave that way. They had other plans and they didn't want me to interfere. The broad with the big booms blinded me.

It was useless to fight back. I was literally swamped by the five broads. They had my arms spread-eagled against the wall, my thighs locked in their arms. To make it worse, the bronze stud joined the jailers and, smiling, planted himself right next to my side, already making with the eyes at my crotch. He didn't give a damn what his playmates were up to.

I did. I craned for a look.

What they were up to was a mass gang bang of Brigitte Lebeau. When she realized finally what was happening, she tried to climb down off the hassock and run. It was too late. Every other woman left in the room, led by the lanky Chinese girl, engulfed her. There was a great tearing of clothes, a ripping of the spangles and the feathers and pretty soon, Brigitte Lebeau was exposed in all her feminine glory. For a moment, the attackers admired her, giving her the tribute of their *oohs* and *aahs*—remember Naadia Grey in *La Dolce Vita*—the orgy scene? Well, Brigitte had all that and more. She was as finely figured as a woman can be. Her body was a gorgeous arrangement of hill and dale. The valley was as inviting as a Venus mound can be. Danielle's doll of a mother even had dimpled knees.

There wasn't a thing I could do but watch. And that hurt too. The bronze stud was admiring me by this time. I was helpless and he was making measurements with his hand spans. I didn't care. I tried to beg them all to stop but one of the broads had stuffed a spare bra into my mouth. It was silk and it tasted lousy.

Then it began.

Maybe a dozen women, I lost count, spread Brigitte Lebeau on the carpeted basement floor and got going. They hit her from all directions of the Lesbian's compass. The North, South, East and West of Madame Brigitte was assaulted and the ground was held by one ravening, ravaging female pussycat. For a second, the tableau was a weird wheel of passion with Brigitte the hub of the spokes. And then the scene revolved and the biting, and the eating and the drinking began. What a feast for a pervert! And playmates of sex clubs all over the globe.

And those sounds, the telltales; the squishy, slurping, gurgling, echoing rhythms of evoked passions. Madame was only human. She tried to fight. Her mouth broke free for a moment and she shouted, *"Damon, I am destroyed!"*

She said a mouthful and got one too. The lanky Chinese whose breasts were not lean, rammed her right breast into Brigitte Lebeau's mouth to silence her. After that, it was all of a piece. The grunting and the groaning, the twisting and the turning. The Madame was only human, after all. She began to enjoy herself. Enjoy? She went ape. When every opening of the body, when every inch of responsive flesh is titillated, it would have taken a Saint to resist and even then, who can really say?

The Madame was being reamed, steamed and dry-cleaned. Almost renovated, you might say, and the dry-cleaning job was being done by the sort of dames who make their living at it. I looked away but the smacking noises would not go away. The room reeked of the aroma of intercourse. Maybe not too heterosexual but what the hell. Brigitte Lebeau was fighting back, biting back before they ruined her altogether for a man. Any man. Will power in sex is a vastly overrated and very much misunderstood item of make-up. Nobody's *that* safe.

Madame Brigitte Lebeau was being seduced.

She was being raped.

She was being devoured.

Wolfed, ravaged, ravished and humiliated. By a pack of the horniest, most lecherous, most self-serving bunch of female cats I have ever personally witnessed in action. To my shame and lack of action.

What could I do?

What did I dare do?

The mad little mob scene taking place in the very heart of the hole known as *Les Deuces* was one of those tidbits which was meaningless in a world like this one but it just could be the sort of soul-shattering situation and experience from which a woman like Madame Brigitte Lebeau might never recover.

I had to do something.

Anything.

70

Desperately I gazed around the room, blotting out the wicked sexy scene before my eyes. Looking for a way out, an answer to a horny dilemma. Madame Lebeau had about five more minutes before she became the very looniest of dames in all of France. You could only take so much, be used so much before the wheel will spin the other way. I know. Don't I major in the understanding of the sexual condition as it applies to the human race?

Under Paris skies, a very heterosexual woman *could* be converted into the most free-wheeling Lesbian in the universe.

Especially sensual, liberated women like Madame.

How much can any woman—any man—really take when the lips are down?

The bronze stud, all curly-haired and smiling, breathed in my ear. "Hah. I am fully a thumb longer than you. See?"

"Congratulations. Buzz off."

He ignored me, chortling to the panting wenches that held me captive, women waiting their turn at the festival of Brigitte Lebeau. The crossword-puzzle beauty was champing at the bit now.

"See? He is not all they say! I beat the American! I, Michel-Duval Fountainbleau!"

The girls ignored him too. They were beginning to change places with exhausted members of the love pack trooping back from Brigitte's much-abused body. I closed my eyes. I didn't want to look anymore. I was close to panic too. What if the party got around to me? Ouch. That would really hurt. A castrating process, psychologically, for a man like me. The boys with long hair were clapping their hands, agog.

We had to get out of there. Pronto. Or the world might see the very last of healthy, normal sex treatises by one Rod Damon. I did not want to be the laughingstock of a lousy little sewer called *Les Deuces*. So I gambled. I opened my eyes and smiled at the bronze stud. He smiled back proudly.

"Think you're pretty good, eh? Well, I've got news for you. I don't even have an erection. What do you think of that?"

71

His face broke apart. "That is ridiculous!"

"Yeah? Would you care to challenge me in the center of the floor?"

"But—but—" His eyes wouldn't leave my tool. "Even now you are thrust out. At the ready. Am I a fool? My own eyes tell me that is about as far as you can go . . ."

"What's the matter, Michel-Duval Fountainbleau, are you afraid to be shown up in front of these whores?"

"Afraid? I?" He snorted and I swear he would have pounded his chest like Tarzan. I had insulted his manhood.

"Then turn me loose and let's see. To hell with my friend. She's having fun, why can't I?"

Hoarse shouts and moans were emanating from the fleshy pile of bodies in the center of the room. The bronze stud waited no longer. He stepped back, tugging me free from the women who held my arms and legs. He flung them away like so many toys, literally dragging me out to the center of things. By that time I had all the freedom I needed. Nobody in the daisy chain snaking around on the floor paid any attention to me and the bronze stud. And that was all the operating time I needed.

I kicked him right in the balls. High and hard. There was no time to be a nice guy. He went down, screaming, pawing at his most prized possession and rapidly forgot about everybody else in the world. That's what I wanted. I moved fast.

The drugged, sexy bitches swarming over Brigitte Lebeau never saw me coming. I kicked into the pile, scattering naked whores right and left, kicking them where it would do the most fun and dug Brigitte out from under the pile. It wasn't easy. She was a battered, limp, nearly lifeless bundle of womanhood. I swung her in a fireman's carry over my shoulder, turned around and lowering my head, charged through the room for the stairs leading up out of the sewer sin circle. I stiff-armed Miss 50's out of my path. She went down with a meaty bounce, landing knockers first.

Mad angry screams rose in a chorus behind me.

The Chinese sweetheart tried to block me. I let her have one right across the chops and she went down with a silly smile on her face as if she liked it. By that time, whatever customers were left in the joint were shrinking

72

back from me, trying to stay out of trouble. I shouldered through the pack, racing like mad, until I gained the stairs. The bronze stud was sitting on the floor, huddled over his joystick, crying great tears. Brigitte Lebeau's shapely sack of flesh was getting heavier by the second. Some shouted, "To arms!"

Up under the manhole cover, the doorman, a burly, hairy cat with big hands, tried to block me at the ladder. I flung a thick roll of franc notes in his face and he immediately closed his eyes, turned around and lay down on the floor as if I had hit him. Damn clever, these doormen. And money can always *parlez-vous*.

Getting through that manhole cover was like coming back to life. The air was sweet, the sky was full of stars and not even a passing *gendarme* marred the view. The cops had to be on the take. Nobody runs a spot like *Les Deuces* without an official by-our-leave. And some loot. The way of the crooked world. I was in a rotten mood. As hard as nails and unhappy.

I found a cab, poured Madame Lebeau into the back seat and gave her home address to the cabbie. He was a French cabbie. A badly mauled naked female meant nothing to him. Other than as a curiosity. I was breathing like an old locomotive, realizing how narrowly I had escaped a mass bungholing and God alone knew what else.

"*Madame* is ill?"

"You'd be too if you'd been attacked by a gang of alleycats."

His eyes were kind and interested in the rearview mirror.

"Two-legged or four-legged, *Monsieur?*"

"Real mean pussies. The worst kind of people."

He sighed and gave his wheel a flick. He was a man's man.

"It is true. One can suspect what a man will do but no one can safely say what a woman will. Ah—the world is in sad shape, my friend. Is it any wonder that the Peace Talks can not be settled?"

"Yeah. Ain't it the truth."

Brigitte Lebeau was stirring against my shoulder, moaning and crying in her delirium. I checked her quickly. She was Hickeysville, France. Large red strawberry bites cov-

73

ered every inch of her anatomy that I could see. Especially around the thighs. They had done her up red-black-and-blue as well as brown. What a sorry sight she was.

I was disgusted. Even her dimpled knees were gouged.

The investigation, which had been running along smoothly, had run afoul at *Les Deuces*. A complete dead-end—well, not really *dead*—and a waste of time. Finding a murderer had nothing to do with getting raped and mauled in an underground bistro. I felt in my side pocket for Danielle Lebeau's address book. *It wasn't there.* I cursed. It must have dropped from my pocket in all the fandango accompanying the hasty exit from the place. That—or it had been lifted from me during the assault on Brigitte Lebeau. I had to think about that. It was a screwy possibility.

Maybe *Les Deuces* was not what it all seemed at first glance.

Maybe Danielle Lebeau had had it listed in her address book for a very good reason. Maybe it just wasn't a place to see how the other half lived and tangled tails.

Maybe she'd gotten more than just her thesis, *Sex and Concentration,* out of it.

Maybe—hell. I had to get Brigitte Lebeau home first and into a hot bath and safely tucked in bed. I'd damn near come getting the beautiful warhorse killed. I knew she couldn't have helped enjoying it a little, but that kind of wholesale sex act is not exactly calculated for the saving of wear and tear on valuable, intimate sections of the body. It can ruin you.

She was still mumbling drunkenly when I sneaked her out of the cab up to her room, with my coat jacket around her for a modicum of protection. When I got her into the room and the door was closed, she was sobbing like a baby. I couldn't keep her arms from around my neck as I laid her down in the four-postered bed. She was crying terribly and her warm hands, scratched and red, were imploring me for something far different than she had had.

"Ah, Rod—please, please—don't go—you must stay with Brigitte. You must make love to me!"

"Look, after what you've been through!"

"That's it! That's just it! Damn me for a wicked woman, I enjoyed myself! You hear? I loved all those hungry

74

mouths, those fingers, those lips—Rod, you must help me! I must find out if I can still enjoy a man. Now, tonight, here—this next second! If those women have robbed me of my greatest delight, I will seek them all out with a carving knife and cut their asses to ribbons!"

She lay back on the bed, eyes begging, holding up her arms. There was a desperate rhythm in her quivering breasts and her straining thighs. I sighed and took off my tie.

"You're sure, Brigitte?" Chewed up, bitten, red-marked and all, she looked like the godmother of every lovely courtesan in history.

"Sure?" Her laugh rose bitterly in the tiny, dark room. A glow of neon filtered from without the narrow windows. "I am sure of only two things. *This.*" She touched the silken convex of her womanhood. "And *that.*" She touched the bulge of my trousers where big things meant a lot. "For a French woman, there is little else in the world. You understand? Ah, Rod . . . give me back my pride and my honor and my soul!"

"If you insist."

"I do insist."

"I warn you. If it hurts even just a little, promise you'll say so and we'll try again later."

"Oh, hurt me, hurt me! I wish that with all my heart."

"You *are* nuts, Madame Brigitte, but you're a damn good-looking woman."

"Yes! Is it not lucky!"

"Lucky for you and for me. I love good-looking women."

"Rod?" She stroked me. "Yeah?" I murmured.

"Please stop talking and take me to bed. Now, this instant, *immediatement!*"

I finally agreed and lay down next to her, tossing my socks into a corner.

"Let me kiss you first. Let me build within you the fires that consume . . . in that way I, too, will have a little breathing time to refill my own desires. . . ."

"Now who's talking too much?"

"Pardon!"

She sighed a little and lowered away, raising the bridge to her warm and waiting mouth.

The sinful scenes of *Les Deuces* now took a back seat.

Madame Lebeau reminded me of Minda Loa. Without the clever and tricky feather. She didn't need the south end of a duck to make me satisfied.

So I waited.

And watched her.

It was a very dangerous and daring experiment in a way. Even I, who have satisfied and endured and comforted maybe a thousand dames, wasn't quite sure exactly how successful I would or could be with a woman who had had her very insides and soul ripped apart by a mob of wolfish brutes. There was no telling whether or not I too would damage the tender and gentle libido that reposes in the breast of all womankind.

"Brigitte, please—"

"Yes?" Her eyes tried to find me above the giant that towered in her palms.

"Please remember. It is not a test. Or a challenge. We will go slow, eh? We have all the time in the world."

"Quite . . . *ahhhhhh* . . . ," she murmured. "It is good to feel the salt of a real man . . ."

"All well and good. Just remember, you don't have to prove a thing. *We* don't have to prove a thing. Agreed?"

"Agreed."

"Good. Now get on with what you're doing and devil take the hindmost."

She laughed lightly. "No, we will save nothing for that rascal!"

Madame Brigitte Lebeau wanted to get the show on the road. You would have thought it was the only game in town, the way she played it.

Too bad the queer darlings of *Les Deuces* weren't hanging around to watch what I did with the Madame and what she did to me. In the very wise words of Pal Joey, if they knew what they had thrown away they would have cut their throats.

The bronze stud would have committed suicide under the Eiffel Tower.

And maybe Madame Lilly de Jussac would have amply understood why her forthcoming purpose to let me give a symposium on Sex to the ladies of *l'Académie Sexualité*, might just be playing with fire. It would have cured her

Lesbianism for all time, at the very least.

Mady Morrow would have understood. Minda Loa, too. And perhaps, dear little Viviane Fresnay.

I'm sure Danielle Lebeau would have understood best of all what her mother and I did under Paris skies in the little room above the curving alleyway.

After all, the young girl who penned *Sex and Concentration* would have been in my corner. Maybe even shouting *"Bravo!"* and *"Encore!"*

Her lovely mother was Sex and I was concentrating.

Paris and bedsprings.

What a combination.

CHAPTER SIX

We made love for about five hours.

If the good Madame had had any doubts about herself, they all dissolved within the confines of my arms and the wide four-postered bed.

Brigitte Lebeau's return to normalcy was a completely painless process. In fact, we had a ball. From quiet beginnings can come great things. We both went slowly, taking all the time there was and nobody was in a hurry to go anyplace or catch a streetcar or a bus. With caution and care as my watchword, and finesse as my long suit, it was one of the happiest experiences in a lifetime of happy experiences.

"*Sacre,*" she whispered, laving me softly and moistly with slow, deliberate encirclements of her pink tongue. "You fill the eye, Rod."

"Is there any other way?"

"*Mais non*, my sweet one. Ah, so prime, so delicious, so grand an instrument of desire. I love it so. . . ."

She showed me how much, lying between my thighs, as I lay back, trying to see the ceiling. My busy little fingers were carefully *finessing* her curves, working gradually, real snail's-pace stuff. I had to bring her back by degrees. Her hot mouth had already taken me soaring into the stratosphere. But she didn't complain or say anything. She just licked away. The Arabesses and the native women of all the pagan cultures get high cards from sex experts when it comes to fellatio but I have never agreed. Any Frenchwoman worth her salt, can match the best of the lip service crowd. Like Brigitte Lebeau, who by design or *naturellement* knew that slowly scouring the scrotum, tenderly laving the penis head and sliding smoothly along the structure of the phallus makes for great joy and fine growth. Nor did she turn away when the golden gates opened and flooded.

I let her do that for about an overly long hour and all I did was gain added vitamins. As for her, her yearning grew apace and her vitality returned, ebb tide at first, then

78

quickly gathering into a monumental eagerness that doubled her efforts, making her scramble above me, searching to find the lost chord. When she found it, she sighed with all the happiness in the world that there is for a woman and softly subsided upon me, widening her limber legs as she did. Finally she began to move, to undulate and wriggle and in that sinuous direction, lay Paradise. Paradise enow.

My fingers had arced her into a wide dark V of lush surrender. Still I waited, letting her salve her battered wound in her own personal way. The healing fluids of our bodies merged and she sighed again, warm and vibrant and fresh as a daisy again. The moment held and she began to sob softly.

I kissed the nipples of her wondrous breasts as she straddled above me. They were prime and fine, a tribute to her grace and class. In a world of thirty-seven-year-old broads, she was all by herself on top of the hill.

"Oh, Rod, my pet . . . my desire . . ."

"Better now?"

"Better? Best! I am the queen of France . . . ah, you *homme* . . . I could eat you . . ."

"Again?"

"Tease!" She put her thumb against my nose. "My body is healed. You were so soft, so *tres* sweet . . . now we must begin in earnest. Yes? I am hungry for you. On fire. You must show me all the things you know, the things you do. I am no longer afraid. You must—how do they say it in your country—ball me, baby!"

"You're sure?"

"Sure! What do you wish to do?"

"Follow me!"

With a quick movement I reversed her, and forgetting Yankowski, I applied some straight Damon to the situation. The down-from-the-ceiling ploy with the lady's legs firmly athwart the man's shoulders. Brigitte didn't say a word. She simply cooperated and as soon as I dive-bombed into her interior, there was no more holding her. We became two writhing, pumping dynamos, who somewhere in the process managed to fall off the bed, reach the floor and end up near the windows. In the glare of the neon, I showed her how to do The Crab, The Snake

79

and The Monkey's Uncle, rather animalistic little excercises which are enjoyed by the lower classes all over the spectrum. Still, they have a lot going for them. There are no other positions in all the manuals and secret doctrines that allow for greater proximity between the male and female. Old Arabs and ancient Egyptians had finely different names for these postures but modern technology has reduced them to simpler terms.

The Crab, particularly, drove Brigitte Lebeau wild.

"Oh, Rod—I do not complain, you see—but what in the name of heaven are you doing to me?"

"Scuttling, just scuttling."

"Why does it feel so insanely good and different?"

"Well," I said, breathing hard, for it calls for an inordinate amount of thrusting, "you see, on the floor like this, with you in front of me, and your *derriere* plastered to me, as we go around in semicircles in the sideways *scuttle,* every fibre of your body and mine are trying to mesh while still in movement. See how it feels? Like turning to jelly, like—oh, hell, as long as it feels good!"

"Ah, that it does. Scuttle some more, *cherie!*"

So we scuttled and snaked and finally did The Monkey's Uncle. I'd need a diagram to tell you how that goes, but Brigitte caught on right away. She had no trouble at all straddling me, face to face, as we jumped around the room. The idea of this ploy is to see how long you can keep it up without going wild. Sort of a reverse on the monkey-on-my-back situation. Anyhow, Brigitte reveled in it.

She reveled all night and as the wee small hours entered the narrow windows, we finally made our weary happy journey back to the bed, damp with lover's dew, limp with well-done revelry. She subsided against my chest, dozing off to sleep. I hugged her to me, feeling all of her splendid muscalature welded to me like a silhouette. She was indeed built like a brick building.

"Sleep now," I suggested. "In the morning, we have much to do."

"In the morning," she mumbled, "we will begin again."

I laughed. "Okay. Sleep, and that's an order."

"Rod, *cherie.* . . ."

"Yes, Brigitte?"

80

"I am . . . all cured. I am reborn . . . not even Gaspard's wiggle—"

"Madame, it was a pleasure."

"I will bet . . . you say that . . . to all your Madames . . ."

She fell asleep before I could make a comeback to that. Her warm as toast body made the bed a delicious oven of pleasure.

What could I say after I said I wasn't sorry?

I went to sleep too, watching the dawn come up like a gray fog while a jet plane made a helluva racket in the sky over the hill house. I was trying to make some sense out of *Les Deuces* and thinking of Walrus-moustache's Paris phone number. Maybe it was time to call him.

The peace talks were still going strong, but nowhere did anybody seem to be interested in the knife that had killed Danielle Lebeau. An oriental knife, Walrus-moustache had said. . . .

I was thinking about that when sleep whammed me in the eye and put me out for the count. That dark lady who loves us all.

I never did find out if Madame Brigitte Lébeau snored or not.

Maybe I do too.

Nobody's ever told me.

Small wonder.

When I'm not alone in the sack, I seldom waste my time sleeping. I'm one guy who doesn't believe in sleeping his life away. Shakespeare, notwithstanding.

You can sleep all you want to after you're dead and gone.

What's *goner* than that?

A cock crowed at sunrise. I woke up.

To find Brigitte Lebeau sitting up in bed next to me, her lovely face propped on her right hand as she stared wistfully down at my *raison d'etre*. Her pink body glowed in the gloom.

"You called?" I yawned.

She shook her head admiringly.

"An hour or two is enough to refresh me. I have just been sitting here doing two things. One of which you

81

see—regarding that *fantastique!* of yours. Is it always so, ah, prepared?"

"More or less."

"Much more and you would be a freak. Did you sleep well, *mon cherie?"*

"The sleep of drunks, babies and well-hung men. What's the second thing you were doing?"

She folded her hands. Since she was still as nude as a peeled grape, her breasts arched beautifully. The areolas were rosy red.

"I am thinking of my dear departed dead. And the awful place we went to last night. You recall?"

"I recall. I should think you'd want to forget that queer factory as soon as possible."

"I cannot. I feel as if we missed a clue there . . ."

"Maybe but we didn't miss any bets. Look, I hate to impose, but how's the food in this place? I am famished. I think I got through nearly all of yesterday without a decent meal except for all that minor nibbling we did in the bistros where we checked on Danielle's address book. Which reminds me. It's gone."

"Gone?" Her eyes popped. "How can that be?"

"Lost, strayed or stolen. Take your pick."

"I pick *stolen,"* she vowed triumphantly, "at *Les Deuces!"*

"So do I. But feed me first before I eat you raw and chew you into little pieces. . . ."

"I would like that," she confessed. "I am shameless."

"Ain't we all? Food, Madame, *please."*

She laughed. "With ketchup on?"

"Anything. Only hurry, woman, hurry!"

The morning light revealed no telltale signs on her face. Not so much as a wrinkle. For thirty-seven, she was holding down the fort better than Custer had.

She fed me. A loaf of pumpernickel, three cups of coffee to wash it down and generous slabs of Camembert cheese as well as an apple or two. It wasn't a blue-plate special but it was food. I devoured it all as if it was pheasant-under-glass. I skipped the cognac. The coffee would have to do me and it did me fine.

Brigitte didn't eat at all. She was far too happy having rediscovered her femininity. In fact, she got downright coquettish. She kept on eyeing the four-poster. Longingly.

"Later, Brigitte. We have too much to do. Rome wasn't built in a day, you know."

"With you it seems so," she laughed again. "What will we do this morning?"

I was about to come up with something brilliant when my eye suddenly caught a reflected gleam of light from the far side of the apartment. For a moment, I blinked and then I got up slowly from the table. Brigitte's eyes followed me with curiosity, for I must have had a strange expression on my face. I hadn't noticed before but one of the light fixtures on the wall which faced the bed was flickering, glowing strangely. I looked at the windows. There was no sunlight. Which didn't make sense.

Quickly, I skipped to the wall and studied the light fixture. It was just about six incles above my head and I had never seen a light fixture like it. It was a huge bracket affair about six inches square with a mirrored insert. Above this was the light bulb poking from its socket. I stared at the mirror. It was a curious place for a mirror. How many six feet six people are there? I looked back at Brigitte Lebeau.

"How long has this been here?"

"What?"

"The mirror? This bulb?"

"Eons. Since I have lived here. Why?"

"Crazy place for a mirror, isn't it?"

She shrugged her shoulders. "Architecturally these homes are not all they should be. But come—why is it so important?"

I couldn't be sure but I've seen two-way mirrors in my time. There was no other explanation. This one was set in the wall. The bulb and its bracket was poking out on an elbow of metal. I took the gamble, risking being thought a maniac.

I got a stool, stood on it and spoke directly into the mirror. Brigitte thought I'd lost all my marbles but I did what I wanted to do all the same. A gamble but some of them do pay off.

"If you can read my lips or hear my voice, you're a dirty peeping Tom. Or Thomasina. Which is it?"

I waited. There was no answer.

"Come on. I know you're in there and you watched us make love all night. Okay. You don't come out or answer, I'll come next door and pull you out by the ear. What's it going to be?"

Again I waited. This time there was an answer. A woman's low voice, reedy, probably funneling through the light fixture, said with a low laugh, *"You are a great lover, Mr. Damon. Can you blame us for watching?"*

"Us? You're not alone?"

"No. Françoise is with me. We live here."

I looked at Brigitte and the utter amazement in her face convinced me that she was no part of this scheme. It seemed that the mother of Danielle Lebeau had been watched for a long time. As well as her beautiful visiting *Académie* daughter. The plot was thickening around the curves. Two-way mirrors yet!

I wasn't going to talk to a light fixture all day. I rapped on the wall. Just hard enough to sound like I meant business.

"Come in here. I want to talk to you."

There was a pregnant pause. No kidding.

"Only if you agree to allow Françoise and I to sample your delicious self."

"Okay, okay. Let's see what you have to offer. I'll give you ten seconds to arrive." I got down off the stool and smiled at Brigitte Lebeau. "You see? You and your daughter have been under surveillance for all the time you were here. Or at least, since Danielle came back and forth."

"But why? To what end?"

"Isn't that what we're trying to find out? Hush up, now. Guess who's coming to dinner? *Hello* . . . who have we here?"

I should have known. The door swung open and in marched the lanky, slant-eyed Chinese woman and the dame with the size fifty headlamps. They both came in, smiling, almost tiptoeing. Obviously they had no hard feelings about the night before. Slant-Eyes bowed and rubbed her jaw with a grin and Miss 50's placed her hands against her formidable chest. Brigitte Lebeau glowered but I held her back.

"Easy, Madame. These two never laid a man in their lives. All they want is to taste the sizzle but not the steak. Right, mademoiselles?" They almost bowed and started to circle me.

"Françoise and I will help you," the Oriental long drink of ink said. "It is time you realized, Madame Lebeau, that Dany was one of us. That she worked at the club. *Les Deuces.* When you came last night, I was startled to see you. Dany did not want you to know but obviously you did know."

"Mais non," Brigitte shrilled. "I didn't know! You lie! My daughter was not like you."

The bosomy one giggled and reached out to touch me. The Chinese impaled her with an inscrutable look. Then she got back to me.

"Dear Mr. Damon. Françoise and I, as you, are not interested in coition. Therefore if you will allow us to kiss you, we well might tell you what you may like to know about *Les Deuces.*"

"And you are——?"

"Mei Ling High." She pointed at Françoise. "This is my friend, Françoise Marnay. Allow us now to satisfy our curiosity. Through the mirror, we found you hard to believe."

"You hoydens!" Brigitte cried, reaching out. "Get out of my house! He is mine, all mine——"

"Brigitte, please," I begged. "A taste won't kill me nor spoil it for you. Anything that will help find Danielle's murderer——"

She deflated, eyes moist. Sighing, she turned and walked over to an ottoman and sat down. The latent lesbianism in her had once more won the day. And also her true motherly instincts.

"Very well. But only five minutes apiece shall you have with them. Then we will get to the bottom of this mystery. I wash my hands of it!"

"Good." I walked over to the bed and kicked out of my trousers. The miracle whip snaked out and Françoise and Mei Ling High did a double-take. They started to breathe in a funny way but they came a little closer to it. Until they could reach down and touch it. "Don't crowd now," I

85

warned. "There's enough for both of you, but don't get too greedy. We have a business deal to transact, right? A kissing spree for information."

"Yes," Mei Ling High said and lowered her mouth. "But first let me taste they wares, man of the West."

"At your service, lady of the East."

She began to lick. A long, hungry, almost greedy suckling that could have milked a thousand cows. But she was punctual and precise. When Brigitte angrily called time, she bowed, bit me once more and removed herself. Françoise filled the gap. Coming on with low oaths, big red mouth and trying to squeeze some extras in by mashing her mammaries around me. It was ten minutes of pleasure, all in all, and I enjoyed every second of it but I must confess I *was* thinking about the Danielle Lebeau mystery. It was getting deeper and wider than an aged whore's port of call.

Satisfied, the woman moved back. I re-zippered my fly and got off the bed. The dolls were real pros. I was hard as a rock.

"Not bad," I admitted. "You two could plaster cement. Now, down to business." I was very much aware that Brigitte Lebeau had very much enjoyed her role of spectator. She looked glassy-eyed and her thighs had squirmed apart uneasily. But there was no more time for that either. "What's with this *Les Deuces* club and Danielle Lebeau? Her mother and I just don't believe she was your kind of a girl. No offense intended."

Mei Ling High bowed again. She was gaunt but she was real juicy tenderloin. Exotic and Oriental and downright scrutable. Françoise, the bovine blonde, simpered at her side. You couldn't insult her with a dictionary. She looked like the downright dumb blonde species.

"For you answer, Mr. Damon, we will take you to the club. You will meet Annette. Annette will explain all. She is our, ah, employer. A remarkable woman. We can tell you nothing until you see Annette. It was she who sent us to spy on you this time. Annette wants you to *whip* her."

"Who? Me?"

"Yes. She wishes the great Damon to torture and torment her. As only he could and can. That is the arrangement. You must agree to it. Do you agree?"

86

What a weird pickle this was. Queers on all sides and murder to boot. Obviously, whatever answers there were to the Lebeau enigma rested in that underground, manhole-covered paradise for perverts. I took a deep breath. Brigitte Lebeau was on her feet, her face pleading with me to say Yes. She liked living at ninety miles an hour.

"All right," I said. "Let's go. The sooner the better. I would like to get back to the States in time for the World Series."

"Baseball cannot match what you will find at *Les Deuces*," Mei Ling High said in a faraway voice. Françoise Marnay giggled again.

Which is how we all got back to where we started. At the *Les Deuces*. Only this time in broad daylight. Fully dressed and in our right minds. I hadn't had a chance to call Walrus-moustache, nor had I even read a newspaper. But I was hot on the trail and I had the acute feeling that I was getting someplace fast.

Maybe the graveyard.

Maybe not.

But anyhow, I was on the right sadistic track. Any time a lovely doll is murdered with a knife, always look for a twisted mind. Nobody else would ever dream of wasting a prime specimen like Danielle Lebeau that way unless he or she was off the rails.

Catch me killing a woman. Hah.

I think I know a million other ways to knock her off and enjoy myself at the same time.

Brigitte Lebeau was still glowering as we followed the lanky Oriental and the bosomy Occidental down the winding stairs of the house she lived in. Cabbage smells filled the air again.

"Don't trust those hussies," she whispered, "they will cut your heart out if they get the chance."

"Not if I see them first," I said. "Come on. Chin up, Madame. This may be a big help all in all. Annette may have the answers we want."

"So might the Almanac," Madame Brigitte Lebeau said fiercely. "But I do not live by books."

We didn't say another word to each other until we were all crowded into a black touring car which was parked on the slanting hill. Mei Ling High drove, her free hand clasped around Françoise's. Love in the afternoon. The kids were hung on each other. Brigitte snorted again and placed her hands on my lap.

"If they hurt you," she vowed in another whisper, "I'll have their breasts for breakfast!"

What a woman. No wonder France has survived all these years.

If Danielle Lebeau had what she had, that girl might be alive today.

Sans doubt.

With or without ketchup, *mes amis.*

The black touring car reached *Les Deuces* about fifteen minutes later. That is to say, the manhole cover. For daylight purposes, the entrance was camouflaged with one of those MEN AT WORK set-ups that allows for a curtained, roped-off area to block off passersby. The cobbled street, a narrow areaway not unlike Wall Street in New York, was deserted. Again, I didn't see a single *gendarme.* Somebody had a friend at the local prefecture, okay. Mei Ling High slowed the touring car, we all clambered out right above the spot that marked the club and she motioned us to go down while she parked the car.

Françoise led the way. Madame Brigitte Lebeau swayed behind her and then I trooped down too. A flock of pigeons on a roof nearby all cooed in chorus. They flapped their wings as if they were cheering us on. The new day had begun with a lullaby to Birdland.

I had only one regret.

I was kicking myself for not getting in touch with Walrus-moustache. The way things were going, I had the distinct impression that I was getting into a lot of hot water without letting the head chef know I was monkeying around in the kitchen.

There isn't an easier way to get burned.

Ask Julia Child.

CHAPTER SEVEN

The mysterious Annette was waiting for us in one of the twenty cubicles that made up the decor of the club. But this cubicle had a lot going for it. The wall-to-wall carpet was practically knee-deep and there were enough bolsters, cushions and stuffed animal dolls to supply Macy's. Françoise led us to the curtained entrance, giggled, and disappeared. Madame Brigitte sniffed the incense still smouldering around the place, pushed the curtains aside and shouldered in with me on her tail. Nobody else seemed to be around *Les Deuces* that morning. Not the bronze stud, the girls, the customers or even the hairy doorman. Only Madame or Mademoiselle Annette. The leopard skin walls reminded me of the exotic backdrop in the sexy photo that Danielle Lebeau had been so ashamed of. It was a dead ringer.

Annette was seated cross-legged on the floor in the cushiony cubicle. She had a lot going for her too. Raven-black hair, eyes as big as saucers, with breasts to match and a very, very scanty scrap of silk that wound about her torso and hips like a scarf. It was flaming red, and exhilarating match for the lady's green eyes. Also, she looked about twenty-four by 38-22-38. I haven't seen a waist like that since Scarlett O'Hara.

"Sit down, sit down," she said in a low, thrilling voice. "We will all be good friends in no time at all."

I motioned to Brigitte, who was too busy sizing the dame up for queerness to sit down. Madame Lebeau was stilll angry about last night.

"Prove it," I rasped. "Chinatown and the Cow Woman says you can tell us a lot about Danielle Lebeau."

"In time. First, make yourselves comfortable. I am so pleased to see you both. The very famous Mr. Damon and of course, the one, the only, the unforgettable Fifi La Fleur!"

As mad as she was, Brigitte was pleased. Fame is so fleeting.

"Thank you, whoever you are. But come—what can
89

you tell us about my precious daughter?"

Annette patted the cushions next to her side.

"Please sit next to me, Brigitte. I will respect your alias, you see. I simply wanted you to know that I know who you are. I worship your name. You showed the world that a woman is a woman from the very cradle itself." Brigitte looked at me and I shrugged, so she sat down next to Annette. The woman laughed and reached out to hold Brigitte's hand. Her green eyes were on me, though. Exploring.

"Do you wonder why I had you brought here, Mr. Damon?"

"Funny you should say that. I was just about to ask."

"Perhaps I should explain the purpose of *Les Deuces* to you first. As a man of sexual keenness and knowledge, you of all people should appreciate a hostelry like we have here."

"I'm listening."

"Very well." She was eyeing me but stroking Brigitte's crossed thighs now. Madame Lebeau's skirt had ridden up, exposing her dimpled knees. Brigitte did not move away. "*Les Deuce's* doors are open to all who seek the ultimate in sexual diversion. We do not turn anybody away. Not anybody. Homosexuals, voyeurs, bisexuals, even asexuals—whatever men and women seek to satisfy their libido, we provide. You understand?"

"Come to the point."

She smiled and patted her heart with her free hand. It was a heart as big as a house.

"You understand—all men and women are not created equal. You should know that better than anyone. They tell me that you shamed poor Michel-Duval Fountainbleau last night, but no matter. The point is, we must provide for some of the people who come here. Many of them are celebrities, people in the news—government officials too. But we are discreet. The police cooperate with us for a fee and nobody wonders about *Les Deuce*s. Now—as to my reasons for bringing you here. You are in Paris, Mr. Damon, and I would consider it a great honor if you will allow us to throw a grand soiree in your honor. There are many of my customers anxious to see you, to hear you. To—ah—*experience* you. I am willing to pay you any sum you care to name if you accept. There is big money behind me so don't haggle over price. We can meet your price."

I stared at her. But it was an opening, a wedge.

"I promise to think it over. Now, about Danielle Lebeau. What does a girl like her have to do with a place like this?"

Annette now looked at Brigitte Lebeau. She almost looked contrite. Sad, even. *Almost.*

"If Madame Brigitte will consent to beat me, I will tell you. But not until then."

Brigitte shrank back. *"Beat you?* This is nonsense!"

"No, Brigitte," Annette cooed like the pigeons, reaching behind her. She brought out a long black riding whip, tooled in gold. Even in the dim light of the cubicle, I could see the letters *Annette* inscribed on the haft. The same silly thing we had found in Danielle's baggage. "Yes—you recognise this? Danielle was one of us. Indeed, she was one of our best ladies. The customers adored her. I cannot say who killed her, for I do not know. But come—use the whip on me please. I have been flagellated by some of the most famous women in the world. Movie stars, stage actresses, princesses—but I would deem it an honor to be flogged by the woman who was Fifi Le Fleur, Child Courtesan!"

Brigitte glared at her helplessly. Annette was carefully disrobing, without getting up. The flaming scarf fell away and for Brigitte's eyes and mine, there sat a splendidly nubile broad, all flesh and a yard wide, ready for the whipping post.

"Rod—" Brigitte ahemed and ahawed. "What am I to do?" I could see her decency wasn't offended as all that. The taint was still on her. She too liked sex in any form. The shapelier the better. Nobody wants to be over the hill at thirty-seven.

"Aw, crap," I said. "Give her what she wants and then maybe we can find out what the hell this is all really about."

"But, but—"

"Go on. I don't mind. I haven't watched a bare ass get striped in many a moon."

Annette laughed happily and bent over, exposing her buttocks. She had no more to say. She simply wanted what

91

she wanted. She braced her hands against the thick carpet and I marveled anew at the curious byways of sin. The dame had a figure that would drive burlesque audiences nuts and all she wanted to do was have it beaten daily. Like a rug.

Brigitte shuddered, closed her eyes and raised the whip. It came down lightly at first and Annette whimpered. But a few more light ones and Annette went berserk.

"Harder, harder, you fool! That's love-tapping——"

Brigitte snarled an oath and really let her have it. The whip flicked like a muleskinner's lash and Annette shrieked with joy. The shriek ignited Brigitte. In no time at all she got right into the spirit of the thing and whaled away. Annette's bared beauty flattened out, bobbing, thrusting, wanting to meet the lash. After a dozen strokes, I'd had enough. I had to hold Brigitte's arm back. Her eyes had that glassy look again. She could talk against queers all she wanted but she had a streak within her as wide as the Comstock Lode. She liked *girls* as well as guys.

"Okay, okay. Don't spoil the merchandise. Had enough, Annette? That's all you get until I get more information."

She came up, sobbing happily. She leaned back against a cushion, breathing hard. Her eyes held nothing but admiration for the former Fifi Le Fleur.

"Thank you, thank you . . . you see, Brigitte? You see how exciting it is? To whip at beauty, to lash it, to make it scream for mercy?"

"Sure, sure," I agreed. "Now about some simple talking? You have to convince me that Danielle Lebeau was one of you. Can you do that to my satisfaction?"

Annette sighed and Brigitte passed a hand over her brow. She was perspiring. Dew dappled her lower lip. The excercise had put the scent of the bull ring in her nose. The flag was up.

"Really, Mr. Damon," Annette said luxuriantly, stretching happily. "It's a shame that Danielle was murdered, because she held such great promise. She was worthy to be the daughter of Fifi Le Fleur."

"Cut it out," I growled. "Murder's murder. Now are you going to open up in your own way or do I have to . . ."

I didn't finish what I had to say because the curtains behind us parted and in pranced a naked Chinaman, puffing furiously on a short cigar. He wasn't completely naked. A love amulet dangled around his fleshy neck, clattering like beads. But his eyes were angry and his thin falsetto voice rose in an injured whelp. "Annette! You bitch! You've begun without me! You've got your goddamned brass, I must say!" He was shivering with rage, his Buddha-body spilling like jello. "Whose idea was it in the first place to bring them?"

Annette smirked and Brigitte Lebeau threw her hands skyward and crossed herself.

"Shut up, Wan Lo. You're here now, aren't you, and they're still here, aren't they? Control yourself. There's still time."

He ground out the cigar with his bared foot on the carpet.

As mad as he was, he bowed in my direction and had a spare gelatinous bobble left for Brigitte Lebeau. His eyes were shrewd.

"This woman—" he sighed. "Forgive me. Wan Lo, at your service. I'm so pleased you could make it. Annette and I have so many grand plans for you both. Did you tell him about the *soiree?*"

"Yes, I told them," Annette sighed. "Mr. Damon will let us know. Meanwhile—" She held up the whip with which Brigitte had flailed her. "Madame Brigitte has favored me with her love."

"Bitch!" He hissed the word again, fuming, but he still was all smiles for me. "Of course, Mr. Damon, you will do me the honors too? I would deem it a high privilege to be whipped by such as you."

I was beginning to see the light. Beginning to see a way out of some of the dilemma. These two weirdos would make with whip talk all day if they had their way. That's the way it is with cultists. They never stop talking about their favorite subjects. So there was only one thing to do. But I had to do it without Brigitte Lebeau. She was far too *en rapport* with the whole deal. But I also knew I couldn't talk her into leaving. So I did what I had to do. I am a psychologist and a human being in that order. And a Coxeman first, last and always.

"Brigitte," I said and motioned her to me. She frowned, got up and walked toward me. Wan Lo and Annette

93

watched us both, wondering what I was up to. It only took one second.

A short Karate chop to bring on unconsciousness. Not too hard, not too vicious, only a sleep-inducer that a gorgeous self-defense lady had taught me in San Francisco in exchange for some instruction in body holds during coitus.

Brigitte knew I hit her but she never did have time to think about it. Her eyeballs rolled, I caught her before she fell, and made her comfortable on the damn floor, in the corner.

"*Ohhhhh!*" Annette whispered in an awed tone. "That was so lovely. So brutal!"

"Isn't he the beast?" Wan Lo chuckled with admiration. "So vicious and cruel!" He tongued his thick lips.

I had them pegged down to the queer eyeballs but when I have a job to do I do it. I reached down for Annette's personalized whip, flicked it experimentally and turned back to them. They were watching me like mesmerized kids now. Small wonder. I was Santa Claus in their scheme of things and I was coming to give them the hiding of their lives. I managed a leer and pointed to the floor.

"Lie down. *Now*. The both of you. Show me your backsides. You want me to whip you? Well, I will. I'm going to flail you until your flesh is in ribbons, until the blood runs like the Red Sea. Until you beg me to stop. Come on. Get on the floor!"

Delirious with joy, transported by my transformation, they fought to obey, each of them scurrying into position. Annette moaned happily and crouched, spreading her buttocks with her bare hands, the more to enjoy it. Wan Lo shuddered with ecstasy and showed me the fattest ass since Hermann Goering. For a long moment I had to fight my own desires. I really wanted to whip them. But first my plan. There's nothing a masochist likes so much as torture and these two liked their sadists to out-Marquis de Sade. In the dim quiet of the cubicle, with Brigitte out like a light in the corner, I began. Lesson Number One with a Masochist: *Deny* them.

"Now," I said. "Who shall be first, I wonder?"

"Me!" Annette blurted.

"Me! Me!" Wan Lo sing-songed.

94

"Maybe we ought to wait," I suggested. "I think I'll have a smoke first?"

"No!" Annette screamed.

"No! You can't—" Wan Lo began to sob. "It isn't fair. You said you would—you can't change your mind now. Oh, Mr. Damon. Be kind—"

"You mean *cruel*, don't you? Sorry, I've lost the mood. I think I'll go home now."

"Stop!" Annette had whirled but she was still facing me ass-first. "We'll do anything only please lay it on us like a sweet man. Can't you see we need it?"

"Yes," Wan Lo whimpered. "We're sick but there's no other way for us. Be a good man and do your worst. I mean—whip us, for the love of Buddha. Like you promised!"

I could see the perspiration of ecstasy dampening their bodies. They were like dope addicts doing the cold turkey bit. I added some fuel by letting the lash flick out lazily, barely touching them. They both shuddered together like a vaudeville act.

"Nope," I said. "I'm not in the mood. Some other time."

"Please," they moaned, almost in chorus again. "We'll do anything you say . . . only, *please!*"

"Anything?"

"Yes, damn you, yes!"

"Then tell me about Danielle Lebeau and how she died. Do that and I'll whip you so hard you won't be able to sit down for a week."

The prospects of that made them dizzy. Dizzy enough to tell me all I needed to know from *Les Deuces*. They were both so anxious to add to their whip cult folklore that their story almost came out like water. I calmed them down and let Annette do the talking. She didn't turn around, still showing me that gorgeous derriere of hers while her Oriental lover boy listened avidly and added some details, hoping thereby to get some added lashes from a grateful Rod Damon. What a pair of acey-deucies. I think they really swung in all directions.

Danielle Lebeau's fate was a horror story.

Her sexual interests (thirst for thesis material) had led her to *Les Deuces*. She was fascinated, of course, but too beautiful. The inner circle of the club, of which Annette

95

and Wan Lo seemed to be big wheels, seduced her. They drugged her, got her photographed in the nude, blackmailed her with that so she had to come back to them, for fear of being booted out of the *Académie Sexualité*. Madame Lilly de Jussac would have flipped her lid, it seems. The rest of the game got easier. More drugs, more connivings and poor Danielle found herself a member of the Maso-Sadist League, complete with boots, customers and her very own little whip. And then a very important man who patronized the club fell for her in his own queer way. He was as useless as a de-sticked man can be but he got Danielle to accept his passion via the dildo route. Alas, the dildo he used was about the size of a donkey. To hear Annette tell it, he had nearly driven Danielle insane with the thing.

"This very important man," I snarled. "Might that be one Gaston Corbeau, the kindly old father image?"

"Then you know?" Annette looked sulky. "Why bother then with all this talk? Come—whip my ass." She stuck it almost in my face.

"Sure, *cherie*. Tell me more first."

Wan Lo snorted like a steam whistle. His fat buttocks quivered, waiting for the lash. "Hurry up, you bitch! Tell the man what he wants to know! He's one of us, can't you see that?"

Annette had little more to tell but it was enough to freeze the nuts and bolts off a robot.

One last session for Danielle Lebeau, among her crazy queers and the cultists of the club. Drugged again, half out of her mind, she was literally abused and misused by every male and female member of Annette's cult. Real fun and games. And then finally someone had sat her down on his naked lap, stuck the knife into her heart and let her twitch her life out on his erect penis. The Marquis de Sade did that once for kicks with a young boy and it's a famous example of how sick this old world has been sometimes. The body had then been parked back at the *Académie Sexualité* and nobody in Paris had ever connected it with a sex club, peace talks or anything. Just a murder, it says here. I felt like throwing up.

"Who killed her?" I rasped.

Annette's naked shoulders shrugged.

"I do not know. That particular night Wan Lo and I were at the cinema. No one in the group will talk either. It is just one of those things. And those things happen. *C'est la guerre.*"

"Was it Corbeau? After all, he was the one who loved her, wasn't he?"

"He too was not there at the time. He was busy with his fine government work."

"Everybody's got an alibi, huh? Nice. Very nice."

Madame Annette smirked. On her it looked like the kiss of death. I had a horrible picture of Danielle Lebeau getting her comeuppance at the hands of sadists, stranglers and just plain garden variety fiends. My blood began to rise.

"Please," Wan Lo whimpered pleadingly. "Be a nice man and start on me. . . ."

"None of that," Annette growled. "Ladies first, you fat pig. Remember who commands here!"

"Oh, you!" Wan Lo pouted. "You're always hogging all the fun. Let the man decide for himself."

The whip began to twitch in my hands. My temperature shot up higher and higher. This gay giggling Chinaman and his French consort were a duet from those private hells we all know exist somewhere. But this one was a lulu. In a class by itself.

"That's all you can tell me," I asked, "and no more?"

"That is all," Annette agreed, lowering her lashes and raising her hips for the lash.

"You're not holding anything back?"

"What is to hold back? A woman died because she was not built or equipped to stand the superior strain that our strange cult places on the human body. It is as simple as that."

"Sure," I said. "A piece of cake, huh?"

"So, my dear Monsieur Damon, if you will proceed to the main event, we shall be delighted . . . ." Her soft, drooling purr was like a combination of snake oil, molasses and pure acid.

The whip danced in my hands and I fought back a mad urge to stick it in her where it would do the most good. My skin itched.

"Please stop talking and do what you promised," Wan

97

Lo urged, his fat flesh gleaming with sweat. "This isn't fair, to make us wait like this, oh Honored One."

"Oh, crap," I roared and let fly. I was mad, real mad, and few things have pleased me more in this life than letting those two weirdos have it. Of course, the rub was that I was doing exactly what they wanted. Being cruel and nasty to them was like giving candy to babies. They drooled, slavered, moaned with delight and generally had an orgy of self-satisfaction. Wan Lo was beside himself with glee and two more disgusting fat guys you have never seen. As for Annette, she was creaming with machine-gun rapidity, timing her orgasms with each fall of the lash. By that time, I was seeing green, purple and orange. I flung the whip aside in disgust and drew back. I raised my right foot and the same great toe that used to deliver the football for dear old Denver did its best to dropkick Annette and Wan Lo through the goalposts of the leopard-skin walls.

There was nothing more to do at *Les Deuces* and certainly nothing more to discuss. I again had the feeling that Walrus-moustache had erred and all this Lebeau business amounted to was a nasty little sex murder. Aberratively speaking.

As Anette and Wan Lo howled their joy, I scooped Brigitte Lebeau over my shoulder and for the second time in twenty-four hours (or less) I carried her out of *Les Deuces*. On our way out, we passed Mei Ling High and Françoise lying on a chaise lounge of some kind in the murky environs of the deserted place. What they were doing requires no translation. In French or Chinese. Or any other part of the world. Simply it was, you-be-the-six-and - I'll-be-the-nine-and-then-you-be-the-nine-and-I'll-be-the-six. They were smacking all the lips they had.

Mei Ling High was on the bottom. Her sleepy eyes opened as I stalked by, carrying Brigitte Lebeau.

"Leaving so soon?" she purred.

"Go back to sleep, doll. I'll catch your act the next time."

"Very well." She closed her eyes and continued with her work. Françoise giggled. She was always giggling. That great brain. She carried her intellect between her thighs.

Up above in the clear clean world, the fog had thickened. But it was good to get out. I started to look for a cab. Madame Brigitte was getting heavier. And I had a lot to tell Walrus-moustache on the telephone. Like give me my hat and let me get out of Paris. I was wasting my time. There were good books to be written, there was my work in the university and I didn't really care if I ever saw the *Académie Sexualité* ever again. The murdered pussycat had soured me on the whole deal.

I didn't need a cab. A snappy little Renault wheeled around the corner into view and skidded to a stop just in front of me. I gaped and then gawked. The man wearing the bowler hat behind the wheel with moustache drooping was my friend, mentor and employer, Ye Olde Walrus-moustache.

"Lordy, Lordy," I hollered, "how the hell did you get here?"

"Get in," he snapped, flinging the door wide. "With your lady companion. I thought you'd never come out of that hellish place."

"You mean you've been waiting out here all this time?"

"Damon, do obey me, old sport. There's no time to dawdle. I've really no business being here like this. Headquarters would have my scalp if they knew."

"Then to hell with you. We'll catch a cab."

"Really, Damon." He was about to panic, looking to the left and right, up and down the street. "This is still hush-hush!"

"Sure it is but you're just the guy who's going to tell me what is going on. Check?"

"Check! Now will you have the decency to get in?"

"Okay," I laughed. I gave him Brigitte Lebeau's address. "Let's park Madame and have a heart-to-heart talk. Or your Peace Mission is for two other guys, not me."

He nodded, cursed, and shot away from the curb in high gear. His bowler hat was rammed down over his forehead and his mood was ugly. I didn't care. Once again, he had dumped me into the soup and held back the spoon until he wanted to give it to me. What a recipe for business!

The Renault zipped and zoomed through the crooked Paris streets. Walrus-moustache drove like a skilled hackie. I huddled Brigitte Lebeau against me. I hadn't learned too much in two days but I had learned a very important bit of information, apart from the Lebeau case.

Madame Brigitte snored.

And she had had a daughter who simply had drifted into the wrong crowd and gotten hurt in the process. Very hurt. Like dead.

What the hell could the Thaddeus X. Coxe Foundation do about private messes like that?

Nothing, if they asked me.

It's a different kind of peace problem altogether.

"Aren't you going to apologize for sending me on this wild gay goose chase?"

He stared straight ahead but he spoke softly and carried a big stick.

"You fool. This is neither wild and it is certainly more than gay. You will learn shortly that you have just stepped out of the place that is the very core of your assignment. I congratulate you for discovering it on your own. Good work, Damon."

"What good work? Any queer and every queer in the world goes to *Les Deuces*. Big deal. What does it have to do with the peace talks and my assignment?"

"Everything."

"Prove it."

"I shall, but before we talk this thing out I will tell you that you have located the very ring of spies and agents who are doing their utmost to sabotage the conference here in Paris."

I got sarcastic. "How? By killing one little misguided French girl?"

"No," he muttered, "by taking pictures. Miles and miles of film that will soon be produced to scandalize the world and kick the peace talks right in the teeth. Think it over. When you have thought, we will discuss it sanely and sensibly."

"You held out on me again," I rasped. "You knew something I didn't, you bastard."

"Of course," he agreed amiably. "After all, who's working for who?"

I shut up. He had me there. And I had just remembered Danielle Lebeau's coded message sent to the Coxe Foundation for one Rod Damon. I just hadn't been thinking at all. I told you. I'm a lover not a spy. Or a detective.

Walrus-moustache had read my mind again.

"I'm afraid you're truly a lover, not a spy," he sighed. "Be the death of you yet, Damon."

"For once I agree with you."

"Bully for you."

Madame Lebeau snored on, hugging me in her sleep. Walrus-moustache looked pained but said no more. The Renault raced on, finding the cobbled streets of Montmartre. The fog was lifting. A weak sun shined down. I didn't feel very much smart at all. Fact is, I felt dumb. Maybe my brains were between my legs, just like that blonde dope, Françoise Marnay.

"Would you like a bar of chocolate, Damon? There're some Milky Ways in the glove compartment." It was just his way of being kind.

"No, thanks," I muttered. "I'm eating already."

"And what are you eating, might I ask?"

"Crow."

It tasted awful.

For a guy who was usually on a straight meat diet, it was a starvation routine.

Nobody needs protein more than I do.

CHAPTER EIGHT

Madame Brigitte Lebeau was still pounding her ear when we got back to her domicile. So I made her comfortable on the four-postered love bed and covered her with a blanket. As my Walrus-moustache sniffed around the place, I unearthed the bottle of cognac and poured us a couple of drinks. My employer removed his iron hat for once and we parked around the table in the lean-to and talked things out. It didn't matter that I didn't want cognac. I had to wash down the lousy taste of stupidity in my mouth.

"All right," I said after a swig that took the enamel off my teeth. "Give."

"You wish to know all, is that it?"

"I wish to know all, that's it."

"Very well." He wiped the moistness from his scrubby adornment. "We have all downed tools and come up with a few answers. Lord knows how long these peace talks will continue, but if they are to continue we shall have to move fast. Trouble may break over our heads any old time now."

"Stop talking in circles. Give me some facts."

"Very well. Facts. It seems our old friends the Red Chinese are behind this scheme to shame the peace-talks people with luscious sex scandals. They have complete dossiers on the Viet Cong and North Viets representatives; which is to say they know their men and have exploited them. All men have weaknesses and *Les Deuces* is the tool the Chinese Reds are using to make their foul schemes come true. In effect, they have privately bank-rolled this perversion palace to suit their own ends. Are you following me, Damon?"

"Loud and clear. Continue."

"So then. They have taken many many films of these ambassadors and men of good will in their cups, as it were. The more perverted the better, you see. Orgies of sex, sadism, the most barbaric deeds. Now they want more explosive material with which to dynamite the conference.

They want to include France in the three-cornered scandal. When they do—*voila!*—they will expose the filthy footage, send it to heads of governments all over the world and the peace mission will crumple. Who will take seriously men who come to save the world and indulge their nighttimes in orgies?"

"Who, indeed?"

"Now—to make this incident international, they had chosen some willing and immoral ladies from the *Académie Sexualité* and there was to be a filmed orgy with a handful of French officials to make the thing stick real good."

"Such as Gaston Corbeau?"

"Precisely. He is the liaison man for the French ambassador. But plans went awry. Danielle Lebeau got wind of the scheme, was dragged into it, thanks to Corbeau's peculiar fetishes, and, sadly, was killed when one of the perverts let his worst nature get the upper hand. They want a sex scandal; *not* a murder party. That changes matters. So you see, the 'incident' is still on the menu, as it stands. Danielle got the message to us in time but too late to save her own life."

I thought about that and got mad again.

"Did Corbeau kill her? According to what I know, he once used a giant dildo on her."

Walrus-moustache shuddered. "Afraid not. Oriental knives are more the speed of the Chinese. There's a fat official who is particularly corrupt and who is involved in all this——"

"Don't tell me. Wan Lo, by name?"

I had topped him. His eyebrows rose. "And how do you come by that timely name?"

Briefly I told him what had happened at the club before I vamoosed. He eyed me sadly throughout the whole tale.

"Damon, Damon. They lied to you. Madame Annette is a notorious liar and Wan Lo is very probably Miss Lebeau's murderer. Still, we need proofs."

I was thinking even as I downed the rest of the cognac. Brigitte wasn't snoring any more on the bed. I flung ı glance toward the inner room but she wasn't stirring either. Not yet, at any rate.

"We can't let *la belle France* down," I said. "Let's make like Lafayettes."

He shrugged. "The road leads back to *Les Deuces*. I don't see what we can really do except sit tight and wait for a leak of some kind. It's unfortunate. Our hands are tied now, really."

"No dice. I'm going back to the *Académie Sexualité*. I made a few contacts there. I can learn something. Besides, Coxeman representative, did you know that your subsidy is being run by a broad no less queerer than dear flagellating Annette?"

"Lilly de Jussac?" His smile was a sneer. "Of course. We are aware of that too. Reports do get back to us. Perhaps there is a connection with Red China but we haven't found it yet."

I was amazed and told him so. "You let a stainless steel Lezzie like that teach sex to a bunch of innocent young things? You ought to be ashamed. The Foundation ought to be ashamed. *I'm* ashamed."

"Damon." He sighed again, shaking his head. "Do leave the espionage to us, old sport. We are simply giving Madame de Jussac enough rope to hang herself. We thought perhaps she would provide a link to all that has happened. Including the Lebeau murder. You see? So far we have no evidence other than her—ah—queer tastes."

"Yeah, I see. What the hell did you need me for then if you knew all this?"

He almost snickered. "You're not serious? Why, your greatest strength and value to us is that incredibly long, infernally insatiable secret weapon of yours. We knew you would draw flies. And you have. You drew out Madame de Jussac yesterday, spent a rather fine time in the broom closet—I think it was with one Mady Morrow—and you even managed to make a date with another *fille* named Viviane Fresnay. Also, you quickly made your way to Madame Lebeau's, took her pub-crawling, staged a fiasco at *Les Deuces* and then returned today for an encore performance of sorts. Shall I say more?"

"Yes. Who's your other lousy spy?"

"Let us say that the Coxe Foundation is served by many people. However, we aren't all clairvoyant. Some of the material came forth this morning when a bronze giant named Michel-Duval Fountainbleau staggered into a police station demanding to be locked up so that he

104

wouldn't kill himself. When pressed for details, he told the officers all about how the great American Rod Damon had shamed him before his friends and co-workers in *Les Deuces*. That's how it is, Damon. We get reports, calls and details and we piece it all together. Indeed, Fountainbleau, like myself, was absolutely incredulous about the state of your equipment."

"He'll have to stand in line," I growled. "All right. You know what's going on and you know who's responsible. What do we do now? We can't just sit and wait for your incident to explode, can we?"

"No. That's where you come in again."

"I'm always interested in coming in. What did you have in mind?"

"You named the play yourself. Go back to *l'Académie*. See your contacts. Perhaps you can get a lead."

"I am supposed to give a symposium for Madame de Jussac. I also half-promised that screwy Annette that I might attend a big shindig at *Les Deuces* that she wanted to throw for me at some later date. Say—are you thinking what I'm thinking?"

"Capital." He glowed like a light bulb. "Yes, there are possibilities. Let me think. Yes, yes—perhaps you can arrange a party of your own and take pictures too."

"Your ESP is working fine, Walrus-moustache."

"You begin to understand me, Damon."

Just as we were both wrestling out the angles in our own minds, Madame Brigitte Lebeau sleepwalked into the lean-to. She was tousled with sleep and naked as a jaybird. Walrus-moustache eyed her slowly up and down and twirled the ends of his moustaches like an old Prussian Colonel. I told you he wasn't all bad.

"Rod—" Brigitte murmured. "Why did you hit me like that? Did you think I was one of them with their love of cruelty?" She yawned sleepily and her chest muscles flexed wondrously well. She epened her eyes wide, saw Walrus-moustache and didn't miss a beat. "And you, *sacré!* Are you one of them too with that awesome nose piece? What do you do with it—tickle their derrières?"

"Introduce us, Damon," Walrus-moustache purred with great aplomb. "I should be delighted."

I made the introductions and Brigitte Lebeau, who had

crammed a lot of living within an overnight period, yawned again and trotted back to the bed. Before she left, she said, "Come to bed, *cheries*. We can talk much better while we make ourselves more comfortable, yes? Brigitte is *soooooo* tired. . . ."

Walrus-moustache was shocked. He does lead a rather sheltered life.

"Does she mean what I think she means?"

"You'd better believe it."

"The two of us? *Ménage-à-trois?*"

"She's a Frenchwoman. The more the merrier."

"How extraordinary. What a remarkable creature. So well—ah—built too."

"Wasn't she?" I had to laugh. He wanted her real bad but was too much of a gentleman to tell me to shove off. He'd never be the type for three in a bed. Me neither. Not when one of the three was another guy, anyway.

"Well, Damon, I'll leave you to your lady. I must be going."

I liked him that morning for some reason. Charity flowed in my veins. I held out my hand. He stared at it.

"What's that for?" he said roughly, suspiciously.

"Give me the keys to the Renault. You will stay here with Brigitte and I will dash back to the Academy. Time's awasting and I've had my three squares real good since I hit Paris. Relax. It'll do you some good. Put sand in your spinach."

His face turned beet-red. He wanted to say No, but he clearly couldn't. The room was inviting, memories of Brigitte's chassis was dynamiting his *libido*. Like I said, she was one helluva piece.

"But—but—but—" He was stammering for the very first time in our association. "If you go, she'll be angry. How can she want me, after having had you?"

"Pooh-pooh. She's a woman. A good woman. That's why she has no psychic scars and can adjust to her daughter's death. You just give me the keys and I'll be back later. This will make a man of you, my son. She's an incredible lay. Try it and see."

"Damon, I—" He was trying to rally, trying to stay an unemotional, hard-nosed boss. But he was crossing his legs.

106

"Keys, please. I'm tuned out now. I can't hear a word you're saying."

There was a rustle of impatience from the dim inner room. "Gentlemen, how long will you keep a lady waiting . . . ?" The voice was low, sultry and if I knew Madame she was really feeling her oats now. Walrus-moustache was in for a treat.

"You see?" I whispered, taking the car keys from his dazed paw. "She'll take us both. Believe me, she'll settle for you. If you tell her I'm coming back. Once you get started, she won't mind, though. I'm telling you. She lives to make love."

"Fantastic!"

He was still mumbling that, tiptoeing meekly into the bedroom as I sneaked out the front door. Before I closed it softly, I heard one more thing—his trousers hitting the floor.

"*Oooolalala!* How sweet of you to surprise me like this, my dear Walrus-face . . . ahhhhh . . . yes, my pet . . . you can do *that* again. And again . . ." Pretty soon there was nothing but muffled sighs and fierce melodies of passion. I couldn't resist eavesdropping.

I pushed aside a moment's jealousy and continued on down the cabbage-smelling stairway. The Madame was the woman I had described, after all. But Walrus-moustache, for all his glib talk and Victorian denials, was a secret screwer. They're always the worst kind. That crowd scores with best friend's wives, minister's daughters and prim virgins.

But what about Madame Lilly de Jussac?

I wondered what kind of man scored with that kind of cold, merciless fish? I didn't intend to go to Copenhagen for a dame.

I intended to find out. Sooner the better before the burning light in my breeches went out.

As I put the Renault in gear in front of the house on the hill, I thought I heard Brigitte Lebeau scream out in ecstasy. But it was only a low-flying crow taking off from a rooftop. His black shadow raced across the sky.

Which made me think of birds and then ravens and then Gaston Corbeau which I knew meant *raven* in French. The old fraud had led Danielle Lebeau to a mean death and I'd

107

better get around to him before he flew the coop altogether. Government biggie or not.

I was busy making up a lot of plans and stories and ideas as I shot the Renault toward the outskirts of Montmartre, looking for the highway that led directly to the *Académie Sexualité.*

Maybe I could kill a few birds with one stone.

A raven, a Lezzie and a whole flock of low-flying Red Chinese hawks.

There seemed to be a rally of some kind going on when I wheeled the Renault into the heart of the grassy green quadrangle buried between the walled-in terra cotta. The green lawns were alive with about a hundred leather miniskirts and white middie blouses. There was a unified stretching and bending of all the shapely fannies and sculptured chests to the soft music of loudspeakers on the cornices of the buildings playing the strains of, so help me, *Put The Blame On Mame, Boys.* Gilda's theme song played in a real low-down, honky-tonk beat. I watched for a few minutes.

Those *Académie* darlings had what it takes and it was going to be taken mighty soon by a lot of lucky boys all over the world. Ah, youth, youth. Looking at them made me feel all of nineteen again and just as horny.

But I had a job to do. I parked the car, strode into the main building again and walked to the Registration Desk once more. I was surprised to see Viviane Fresnay on duty again; it was as if she hadn't left since yesterday. The outfit of skirt and blouse, the long dark hair, the madonna loveliness was intact.

She wasn't reading *Candy* this time. She'd obviously passed it on. Now she had her nifty nose buried in another well-worn copy of *Fanny Hill.*

I chuckled. "You ought to read *The Bobbsy Twins On The Farm,* sometime. Just for laughs."

"Ah, Monsieur Damon!" She closed the book and batted her sad lashes. "You came back. To go to Room three-two-nine? I leave the desk in one half hour, exactly. Or have you come to see Madame?"

"Three-two-nine." I repeated. "I'll be there. But first I

108

have to palaver with Madame. Can I walk right up or do I need a pass?"

"You have free rein, Monsieur Damon. And I shall be waiting for you. Perhaps you will tell me all about the twins and their farm life?"

I grinned. "I could tell you more about Rod Damon."

She blew me a kiss and I warmed myself with that all the way to the steel knotty-pine door that said Madame de Jussac lived there. I didn't knock this time either. I wanted to catch the Madame with her pants down anyway. With her type, it's always best to catch them off-stride.

I hit the jackpot.

She wasn't only off-stride. She was standing on her head. Believe me, she was all by her lonesome, holding down one corner of the big room, by the wide windows, doing some weird kind of Yoga exercise. Her mini-skirt and blouse were draped in an orderly fashion over the chair behind the desk. She didn't see me come in until I was almost on top her. Besides the head routine, she was pushing up and down with her strong arms. What this made the rest of her lovely body do was beyond description. The flaming red Venus mound was like a batch of fireflies rising and falling. Everything else was swinging nicely-nicely too. Especially the twin whammos.

"Oo," I said, "do that again." She had elevatored right in front of me so that her exquisite mouth was at operating level—for me. I gladly pulled down my zipper. She said nothing and her lovely eyes scorned me as she continued her exercise. Her red lips were moving, counting silently. I stayed where I was and slowly allowed my pride and joy to obtrude into the scene. It sprang out like a divining rod.

I was enjoying myself hugely.

As her mouth dropped down and rose up again, I playfully did a bump and grind. I thudded harmlessly against the wall, toying with her. Then I had her bracketed and I lost my head. All of a sudden, the deep oval of her red mouth was directly in front of me. I was beyond all reason and I guess I wanted to see what she would do. I found out. It was a joyful surprise.

She held herself up in a handstand and quickly sucked

109

me into the maw of her mouth. And then every one of her thirty-two teeth bit down. But hard. As juicy as her lips were, the teeth were a different story. I howled out loud and tried to jump back but I couldn't. She had me pinned even though she was the one with her back to the wall.

"Lemme go! You'll ruin me for life!"

She let up on the pressure. Only a little bit. I couldn't hit her because I was afraid she'd bite me in half. She had me clamped tight.

"Apologize," she mumbled. It was hard to hear her clearly since she was talking around the biggest gag since Joe Miller.

"I apologize. . . ."

She laughed. Right around the tip of my soul, she laughed and then her teeth relaxed. I backed away, relief flooding me. I sagged limply to a chair. I felt like I'd been rescued from the jaws of Death.

"Can't you take a joke?" I gasped. "I was only funning with you. . . ."

She snapped out of her head-stand with a forward snap of her superbly conditioned body and came up standing the right way. A velvety sheen of dew barely tinged her glowing flesh. Her eyes shot electricity and murdered me at five feet. Her howitzers had me covered.

"Don't ever show me that thing again unless I expressly ask it of you, Monsieur Damon. Do we understand each other?"

"*Oui, oui*, lady," I heh-hehed. "Just can't take a joke, eh?"

"A weapon like yours is no joke," she said in a flat sepulchral voice. "But no matter—I am glad you returned to *l'Académie.*"

"In a word, why?"

"I need you, Monsieur Damon. But very, very much."

All of a sudden she had gone formal on me.

"For the symposium, you mean?"

"No. To make love to me."

"Come again?" It was too soon after the biting for me to accept what I was hearing.

"Have you no ears, man? I, Lilly de Jussac, head of this august institution, wish you to make love to me. On one condition, however."

110

"What's that?" I was feeling like an awful fool. She had topped me every second I'd been in her presence since I met her.

"I must be allowed to name the time and the place. And the weapons. . . ."

It was screwy. She sounded like she was arranging a duel.

"Sure. Name your own poison. But make it soon, huh? I'm a busy man and my schedule is crowded. There are a lot of women ahead of you, you know."

She folded her arms across her topless body, and that look of sheer icy coldness dominated her chiseled beauty once more. I tried not to get pneumonia looking at her.

"I know," she hissed. "But I will make you forget every other woman you have ever known."

"And how will you accomplish that miracle?" I showed her my own teeth. She was getting under my skin, which is not easy for a woman to do. Any woman. "I've had a full life. I've had every kind of woman there is, every whichway there is. You tell me. What's so special about you?"

She laughed her icy laugh. Her eyes sparkled.

"You Americans have an expression, I believe. What is it again? Ah, yes—'that is for me to know and you to find out.' Isn't that the way it goes?"

"Yeah. That's the way it goes. You drive a hard bargain, Madame Lilly. I have to say yes without knowing the details."

"Where's your sense of danger? Of excitement? Are you not the man who dares all? *Did* all? Don't tell me you have changed your mind?"

I glowered. "Anything you can do I can do better."

"Good. That's the *ésprit de corps* I expected of you. Good man. And now let me get to my desk and give you all the details you need to know."

"Stop stalling. What's the deal?"

"Very well." She systematically undressed me with her X-ray eyes. "Tomorrow, you will take me to a private party at the *Les Deuces,* a club here in Paris. There you will have your answer."

Les Deuces.

Bingo, Jackpot and Game!

111

CHAPTER NINE

Viviane Fresnay wrapped her smooth legs about me, gave one ecstatic push upwards toward the ceiling of her room and then I plummeted merrily into the wishing well. Wishing can make it so but screwing makes it come true. The madonna-like registrar was a fooler, okay. All that Mona Lisa smile but it hid the heart of a wanton. Her little dormitory room affair had become a midafternoon bower of whoopee. Between the two of us, we'd managed to raise some much-needed hell. I needed some fun and so did she. Inevitably she'd gotten bored reading about it.

Obviously.

"Ah," she murmured, catching her breath as I got off her. "That was good. I am so tired of Madame. She can never replace a good firm male."

"You're a bit of a Wurlitzer too, you little minx."

She laughed and plucked some of my chest hairs from the creamy facade of her body. Her long dark hair and saucer eyes were twin assets for any boudoir. Every bed should have a Viviane.

"You did not spend much time with Madame. I had barely got here and you showed up so promptly."

"She simply made me a proposition and then shooed me out. It seems she had about five students to see. Some of you ladies have been acting up. Sneaking little French boys into your rooms. Tsk, tsk. The Madame was quite put out."

"That lez!" Viviane pouted. She turned over on her side and began to play with my toys. Her fingers were cool and clever. "It's a wonder they don't turn her out. But the girls are all afraid of her. And, of course, some of them *like* her."

I pondered that. I was still off base, thanks to Madame Lilly's odd proposal about *Les Deuces*. That shot had come in from left field and certainly upheld Walrus-moustache's theory.

112

"Tell me, Viviane baby. You good friends with Mady Morrow?"

"The very best. Why do you ask? Do you tire of Viviane already and now want a taste of that bigger, bustier female?"

"Says who?" I squeezed her underrated grapefruit and her fingers tightened around me. My temperature shot up about fifty points. She sucked in her breath sharply.

"*Bon dieu!* Again, it rises. You are incredible, Rod Damon!"

"Don't lose your head. Listen. Would you and Mady come to a little private party I'm planning?"

"At *Les Deuces?*"

"Uh uh. This is my affair. Mine alone. I would like to show you and Mady and some other people I know how to really have a swinging time. France is really a backward country, you know."

She shot erect in bed and her breasts rolled. Her eyes shapped at me. She looked angry and downright beautiful. Her soft mouth quivered.

"So. France is backward. And I suppose America is very progressive? Pah! You will note that the peace talks are being held in my country!"

"Look—" I snuggled against her, letting my armament do my persuading for me. "Politics don't interest me. Sex does. Freedom does. Abandon does. Put them all together and they spell the sort of party I want to give. In honor of Danielle Lebeau."

"Ahhhh—" She melted down like butter. "A noble thought. Dany would have liked us all enjoying ourselves instead of hanging crepe. But who else will be at this party of yours?"

While she was asking, I had carefully found her glory spot again. She began to twitch and push most agreeably. I felt like a well-oiled drill. She had boundless recesses in her. Uncharted depths. She was still as brand-new as a girl can be. She hadn't been explored that much yet. She shuddered in appreciation and her mouth bit into my neck. Her own pink tongue soothed the bite.

"I'm going to invite you—" I pushed hard. "Mady Morrow—" I pushed harder. "Maybe the Madame—" I

113

pushed three times and Viviane cried out in ecstasy. "And maybe some other very important people." I redoubled the pumping, priming her with maddening regularity until she once more became a devotee of the Damon school of love-making. When it seemed as if I might stop, she let out a little cry of sorrow and quickly coiled her loins about me until she had me absolutely hung up and pinned. What else could I do but push back? Which was exactly the way she saw things too. In no time at all we were both like a couple of pounding pistons in an engine room. Viviane balled like hell. She didn't know any better.

And she was in a hurry to learn all there was to know. Who could blame her? It isn't every girl that has a Damon walk into her life with his pants at half-mast.

"Tell me how you're going to invite me again. And all the other women you will invite. I so admire the manner in which you emphasize the names—"

So we did that bit again.

And I added all the other names I could think of. You would have thought it was everybody in the French Classified. I didn't leave anybody out. To Viviane Fresnay's great happiness.

"Rod?"

"Hmmmm?"

"Invite Madame de Jussac again. You do seem to push harder when you use her name."

"I do?"

"You do."

"A Freudian slip. Sorry. Very well. Madame—" She was right. In time with the name, I slammed her so far back, she lost her breath and a long, happy cry parted her lips.

After that I allowed a bit more of love into the act. Then, when I had hit oil for the last time, she came up like a gusher. We subsided after that, gently letting the waves of delight bring us back to earth. Time limped to a standstill.

"Ah, Rod," she said in a faraway voice. "Is it always like this with you? Sex, I mean?"

"*Mais oui*, Viviane!"

"Wee?" She laughed again. "I would not say it was wee, at all. *C'est magnifique!*"

114

We never did discuss *Candy, Fanny Hill* or *The Bobbsy Twins On The Farm*. As far as Viviane Fresnay was concerned, all those books were meaningless when it came to real sacktime. She was a smart girl, she would go far. With or without the *Académie Sexualité*.

I slipped out of her room, sneaked down the hall and tried the back staircase. I headed for the closet where the brooms and Mady Morrow were waiting. I knew she'd be there. She was a smart cookie who knew how to time all her activities when I was in the building. With Viviane away from the desk and Madame de Jussac done with me, Mady would put two and two together and get broom closet. She didn't disappoint me. I no sooner knocked on the tiny door but that it whipped open and I was *pulled* in again.

She obviously wanted a quickie. A stand-up jet job. I guess she didn't have much time. She was nude to the fingernails and toenails and before I could get a word out, she got me in. With both hands and then with a wild wriggle of her thighs, she locked me in a standing prison of warm flesh and warmer motions.

She exploded right away so I let her. She was breathing hard and her body felt like it was on fire down below. I couldn't do anything facy with her except provide the key for her lunging lock. She went at me with a vengeance.

"What is this?" I whispered. "A wham-bam, thank-you, sir?"

"Oh, Rod. Sorry. The damn Madame ordered me up to her office in five minutes. Something about my extracurricular activities with you, I suppose. One of the kids must have ratted. To hell with all of them."

"Hey, don't get in any trouble on my acount . . ."

"Don't be a chump. I'd hold hot chestnuts for an hour in both hands for five minutes of your gorgeous tool. Don't talk. Push me some more . . ."

"But I have something to tell you. Viviane says its okay with her but I want you to make up your mind."

"I'm listening—*mmmmm*—would you just push a little at least? Don't make me do all the work." So I pushed and while I was so occupied, I explained to her about the little party I had planned. I would need girls like her and Viviane Fresnay to throw the wild crowd of *Les Deuces* off

115

the track. They mustn't suspect anything. Not anything.

"Wheee!" Mady Morrow was overjoyed. "A party with you? Count me in! Anywhere, anyplace, any time!"

"You sound like me. And listen—I wouldn't mind at all if, when you see Madame, you sort of drop hints all over the place. Who knows? We could cure that lady yet of her lez tendencies."

"Hot damn," Mady exulted in her Chicagoese. "I'd sure like to see that icebox defrosted right before my eyes. See her begging for your stick. That alone would be worth the price of admission."

"I sincerely hope so," I added fervently.

She added some more ferventlys of her own but her five minutes was soon up so she let me out. When she redressed and took off upstairs, I gave her one last long lingering kiss. She liked that, and I did too. I liked her. There is nothing so satisying as a cooperative broad. Even if she is from Chicago.

My plans were shaping up jolly good and when I walked down the quadrangle to the Renault, the one hundred *Sexualités* were now all shimmying and shammying to a loud-speaker rendition of *Ballin' The Jack*. What a routine. They, with their insidious hip-twisting, breast-shaking and rump-dancing, were balling Jack, Tom, Dick, Harry, Charles, Peter, William, Richard and the French Foreign Legion. En toto. It was a fine school, I can tell you. I was all for it, with or without a Lezzie as its principal.

I hurried because I had a lot more fish to fry, planning for my party. I had to beat Madame de Jussac to the punch. We had to have my party before we had *her* party.

On the way back to Montmartre and Brigitte Lebeau and Walrus-moustache, I detoured for a flying visit to *Les Deuces*. There was no time to spare. I ducked down the manhole, found the ladder and descended into the club. Françoise Marnay and Mei Ling High were sleeping off their kicks on the rug in one corner. I padded toward the cubicle where I had kicked the daylights out of Annette and Wan Lo. I had to control myself, knowing that Wan Lo might be Danielle Lebeau's killer, but like Walrus-moustache had said, we needed proof.

116

I expected to find them in because I'd only left them a couple of hours ago and where can rats like them hole up in the daytime except in a sewer like *Les Deuces?*

When I came back, I got what I came for.

For a long second, I had to watch. It was like a lousy traffic accident. Or an exhibit in a freak side show.

Wan Lo was lying on a wooden board just an inch off the floor. I didn't have to look under him. It was a bed of nails and his fat, chubby face was wreathed in a smile of mingled pleasure and pain. Annette was adding her two cents worth of insanity to the entire procedure. She was straddled above him, at the waist, methodically sticking a collection of long needles into his pudgy flesh. They looked like hat pins and she looked like she was sticking a pig. With each jab, she was emitting a howl like a banshee.

"If you're through making love to each other, I'd like to talk to you," I said.

Annette whirled, her eyes surprised. Wan Lo opened his too, craning his neck. Both of them didn't lose a beat. Sweet smiles of delight swept across their faces.

"You came back," Annette cooed. "You darling!"

"You missed us," Wan Lo sighed. "I knew it. See, Annette? I told you a man like him loved being cruel. He is, you know. Oh, so beautifully, marvelously cruel—" He tried to rise, grimacing with his nails-treatment. "Kick me again, pretty please."

"Don't get up. I gotta run. But I did want to invite you both to my party. You're such a pair of experts, as wanton as I am, I couldn't see my way clear having a ball without you."

"A party?" Madame Annette was incredulous. "But that's so chic of you, Mr. Damon. What's the party for?"

Wan Lo shrilled in his falsetto. "Does he need a reason? Let the man have his party, for heaven's sake."

"I knew you'd understand. Can you both be there tonight at say eleven o'clock? I promise I'll wear my hobnailed boots."

Annette shuddered. "A perfect time. With a full moon and a witch's brew. How glorious! Where is the party to be—would you like it here?"

"No, no. This must be intimate. Just a handful of us
117

truly different sort of folk. However, I would like you to bring your most talented help. And of course, should you care to bring along some of your very best clientele—"

I smiled disarmingly. "I'll be frank with you both. I'm preparing a treatise on orgies. A master work—my tentative title is *Orgies in High and Low Places*. You see what I mean. So I would like your help in selecting some of the very *oddest* and best people."

"Then where is this party to be held?" Annette demanded with her hatpins still jabbing Wan Lo. "It would have to be a fairly large domicile."

"I have hired an entire floor of the Hotel Fourchette," I lied. "My personal playground. That large enough?"

"But that is perfect," crowed Annette. In her delight, she stuck a pin very, very lustily into Wan Lo's stomach. He screamed when it entered but his eyes filled with happiness. I backed out through the curtain. They both gave me the screaming meemies.

"Do bring Françoise and Mei Ling High," I said. "They're a swinging pair, it seems to me."

"But of course." Annette was glowing. I was a convert to her twisted way of life and she was envisioning her truimph telling her world that the great Rod Damon had fallen from his throne.

Wan Lo smiled at me from his bed of nails.

"You promise you'll be mean to me tonight, Rod?"

"I promise. I'll pound your poop, Pappy."

He writhed with pleasure. Annette stuck her tongue out at me and worked it around her mouth. Her wide eyes were vicious.

"And I? What will you do to me?"

"Madame, I'm going to go to work on you with a crowbar studded with spikes."

She swayed, almost passing out with the expectation. But she caught hold of herself.

"Eleven o'clock, you said?"

"Be early and stay late," I advised.

They both shrieked with joy. So I left them. Wan Lo on his bed of nails. Annette with her hatpins.

I got out of *Les Deuces* as fast as I could. Places like that really make a guy like me sweat bullets. The really abnormal, the sick, sick, sick, do not fascinate me at all. I don't mind sexual freedoms and liberties but when it's accompanied by hang-ups like sadism, masochism and homosexuality, I am turned off, but quick.

Still, my plans were still going great guns.

Now I had to make quick tracks. Time was running out.

I had a feeling that Madame Annette would bring the bronze stud, Michel-Duval Fountainbleau to the party. Knowling her, the cruelty of the idea would tickle her right down to her sadistic toes. That is, if the poor stud hadn't gone ahead and killed himself.

I climbed out of *Les Deuces*. Françoise Marnay and Mei Ling High were still snoozing quietly in one corner of the darkened club. I had a feeling I'd be seeing them too tonight. With bells on.

But I also hoped that the bait was being nibbled on and that Madame Annette and her secret friends would think it was a perfect spot and a perfect time to work their peace talks sabotage plan that was crying out for fulfillment. They had delayed too long.

I expected to see a lot of VIPs that night at the Hotel Fourchette. Very VIPs. The kind who would be important to the peace of the world but alas, still the common clay that had to have a little sexual diversion now and then.

That's the way it goes, *mes enfants*.

Everybody wants to get laid.

I had to knock to get into Madame Brigitte Lebeau's apartment. The door was locked. I expected it to be. Walrus-moustache is not the sort to let any grass grow under his hirsute adornment. There was no answer until I began to kick the door in.

Then a very sheepish Walrus-moustache opened the door and peered around the dangling chain. That wasn't all that was dangling. His face was ruddy, flushed and glassy-eyed. Sure signs that he had had—was having—a ball. I expected no less of Madame Brigitte Lebeau *alias* Fifi Le Fleur.

"Really, Damon—"

"Crap," I said, walking by him. "Close the door and crawl into your pants. I'm sorry to bust this up but I've made some plans and they won't mean a thing without your cooperation."

"But who is it?" Brigitte called drowsily from the rumpled bed.

"Damon, my pet," Walrus-moustache shouted, stiffly climbing into his clothes. "Really, Damon, you could have phoned or something."

"No phone here and I wasn't going to stand in the street and throw rocks like in the movies. Come on. By the look of you you've really had your pipes cleaned. You ought to be grateful."

"I am, I am. But still—"

"Is that you, *mon* Rod?" Brigitte's voice was louder now.

"Yeah," I called back. "Go back to sleep. Be with you in a jiffy. Sorry but I have to send our friend on an errand . . ."

"C'est la guerre," she said airily. There was a happy note in her voice. Tribute for Walrus-moustache or promised land for me.

With his suit on and his moustache twirled to get the bedroom scraggle out of it, he was his own man again. He harrumped a few times and I handed him his bowler hat. Briefly and quickly, I told him about my party idea. He listened and forgot about sex and Madame Brigitte. But he was still grumpy and out of sorts.

"Capital, old sport. But why my hat and why must I go rushing out into the night?"

"It's three o'clock in the afternoon," I reminded him. "Which will give you about several hours to make the necessary plans."

"Plans? What plans?"

"Dammit, will you listen? I need a whole floor of that hotel for that party. Get me? Which means you have to pull any strings and wires you can to vacate the floor. There can't be any substitute now. I said the Hotel Fourchette, and the Hotel Fourchette it's got to be."

"Fourchette," he said acidly. "That's French for *fork,* isn't it?"

"No jokes, please. We haven't got the time."

"Very well, I'll get in touch with the Consul. Won't be

easy but it's not impossible. What else?"

"Can you get hold of camera equipment? I want real movie sound cameras. The works. But they have to be the sort that can be hidden and not spotted at all. Also, I want one camera manned by a great photographer. The kind who could win Academy Awards. I want what goes on tonight to be shot in the *cinéma verité* style—you know, like it happens, like it is. Close-ups and tight shots and all. The cameraman can't be squeamish about focusing."

He was beginning to get the picture. A crafty gleam came into his eyes. He could see the possibilities.

"I see. Sort of an Andy Warhol-type movie, capturing every belch, fart and what have you?"

"What-have-you is what we want. If Annette and her weird Chinese boyfriend do what I think they'll do, we can do a little blackmailing of our own and save the world for democracy again, dammit. Or peace. Or whatever."

"Damon, I'm proud of you." He shook my hand. "A scheme worthy of Machiavelli and Joe Stalin."

"If it works. And now comes the hardest part of what you have to do."

He shuddered. "I have a feeling I'm not going to like this."

"You won't. But it has to be done. Do you think you can get your hands on about a pound of LSD?"

"LSD!" he shouted.

"Not so loud. You'll disturb Madame. About a few ounces would do the trick, I suppose, but a pound would really cement the deal."

"LSD," he said again. It was a very dirty word in his book.

"Say it all night. But get it. Come back as soon as you get all these things accomplished and maybe you'll have time for another crack at Brigitte."

He stiffened. "Don't be foul-mouthed, Damon."

"Okay, okay. Make love then, that sound better?"

"Much." He turned to the door. "Damn it, you have given me a lot to do. This will take hours."

"That's the idea but you must be all set up by eleven or it's all a waste of time. Got that?"

"Got it."

121

"Now buzz off." I pushed him through the door. He went, grumbling, but he went. The best part of it was that he thoroughly approved of the plan. There was hope for me yet as spy labor. I knew he'd say that in his report to the Coxe Foundation. If we survived this case.

I was tired. I kicked off my shoes, mentally cataloging all the points of my plan. It should work, if Walrus-moustache accomplished his red-tape miracles. Yawning, I walked to the bed and climbed in. Brigitte was awake and listening. I could tell because she made room for me, allowing only one fleshy thigh and her right hand to greet me in the warmest way there is.

For answer, I faced her sideways, anchoring her legs around my waist in that fine old side-saddle method which is probably enjoyed by many more married men than single ones. It takes marriage and at least a long affair with a woman to appreciate the comfort and pleasantness of the position. Most women I know are very fond of that ploy.

The Madame was well-juiced and oiled but I didn't mind seconds or thirds. Brigitte Lebeau was *all* woman. A rare bird indeed. She had enough to satisfy an army of men. Even if she liked girls.

"Rod?"

"Yes, pet?"

She laughed. "He was so kind and droll. Really, a fine man. Sensitive, afraid to hurt, and his moustaches, how they tickled. But—will you not let me come to the party also?"

"It could be dangerous . . ."

"Talk to me of danger? I, Brigitte, who have lived so long and so hard. Pah! I laugh at danger. The only thing I'm afraid of is old age."

"You ain't old . . ." Slowly, swishily, we began to seesaw against each other. A delicious sensation. She was ample and dexterous. And not tired.

"May I come?"

"You talking about the party or le piston?"

"A little bit of both."

"Then you may do both."

She did. With Gallic sighs and Gallic murmurs. Her accent made it all sound so different even though it was the

122

same old side-saddle game enjoyed the world over. They really dig it in America.

I enjoyed myself too.

The Damon way. With bumps and grinds and delirious thrusts and things that went socko in the night.

It was a love-in all the way.

Which is far better than hate humps, spite jumps, gang bangs and any other kind of distorted sexual activity.

It drove Annette and Wan Lo and Madame Lilly de Jussac and shattered Danielle Lebeau out of my mind. And made me forget all about Mei Ling High and Françoise Marnay and whip cults and nutty broads.

It reminded me of Minda Loa, Mady Morrow and Vivian Fresnay. Three tiger lilies of a far different stripe.

So I had planned a party for eleven o'clock. A party to solve the case, save the world, and maybe send me back to America. But I cheated.

I had my party on a four-postered bed on a hilly street in Montmartre with one Brigitte Lebeau. While poor Walrus-moustache ran himself ragged all over Paris making with the arrangements and handling all the details.

I almost felt sorry for him.

Almost but not quite.

"Ah, Rod, Rod, Rod . . ."

"Yes, Brigitte?"

"I think I could love you . . ."

"Don't think. Do it."

"Would you love me?"

"Brigitte—what the hell do you think I'm doing?"

"But this is not true love—this is Sex—a man and a woman—"

"That was a lousy movie and this is what love is to me. A man and a woman."

"Ahhhhhhhhh, now I understand!"

"Bon! Which reminds me—have I ever showed you the Bon-Bon Method. Of course, you need a box of chocolates—"

"There is a box of them on the icebox."

"Real bon-bons?"

"Are there any other kind?" She laughed, squirming out of the bed.

So, she had a box of bon-bons.

123

So, I showed her.

Ogden Nash's famous verse goes: *Candy is dandy but liquor is quicker."*

But that highly clever, educated rogue could not have been talking about The Bon-Bon Method. Of course he meant in his own civilized way that liquor will weaken Milady's defenses so that you might score a little sooner but I have always scorned the tactics of seducing damsels with varieties of hootch. I want my women fully undressed and in their personally prepared mind when I unpack my tool box.

It's all quite simply, really.

Simply place on luscious bon-bon atop each of the four primary erogenous zones. One on the closed mouth, one for each crest of breast and the last smack-dab on target, poised on the Venus mound. Milady mustn't move until she has let you swoop down from on high like an eagle to kiss and munch the bon-bons from her body. I guarantee you that when you reach home plate, you will slide, Kelly, slide—all the way into Paradise.

It's a home run in any ballpark.

A Grand Slam is what you get for your efforts.

Ask the next chocolate soldier you meet.

Better still, ask Brigitte Lebeau.

"You lovable rascal," she moaned, dropping against me. "Now, I am truly destroyed. Defeated by four lumps of candy. *Sacré!"*

"Aw shucks, t'weren't nothin'."

Her mind, for all her *joyeux* sacktime, was still on the party, though. As mine was. As mine had to be.

As she rubbed me down with a hot towel, scrubbing me to refresh and relax me with her brisk, loving hands, we discussed the whole affair.

"You seek to uncover the ones who murdered my poor Danielle, yes? That is your plan."

"Yes. That and the idea that we want your country to get going with the talks. Time's awastin, Brigitte. It's got to be a success."

"Oui. Tell me. You are more than merely a sex fiend, yes? Truly, you are an agent of some kind? A spy working for the United States."

124

"You might say so."

"Then I do so say. Do not fear. Your secret is safe with Brigitte. Ah, intrigues. How I miss them. The court at Emperor Nicky's, the affairs, the amours—"

"Don't cry. Crying's for kids. We'll lick this thing yet."

"Ah, yes." She wrapped the hot towel around the tallest part of me and placed her warm cheek against it. She sighed and her shapely globes teetered charmingly. "That for you I will always gladly do."

You see? I'm not the only one that's always thinking about sex.

Or always making bum plays on words.

Some people can just never get their minds out of the bedroom!

Lollipop time extended itself once more into the wee small hours of the night. The good Madame, as French as Napoleon brandy and De Gaulle's moustache, had come a long, long way down the road to recovery, being her own grande woman once again. I asked her all about the Emperor Nicky and the good old days of court intrigue. Her royal bedfellow had been a real swinger, it turned out. It seemed it was nothing for him to want to go to bed right after dinner and ball till breakfast. A peculiar hunger which a young, willing and wanton Fifi Le Fleur was quite ready to satisfy. It seemed she had a lot of hungers of her own. When she introduced Emperor Nicky to *soixante-neuf*, he was beside himself with joy. She taught him all there was to know about lip service. In the end, the dear regal man declared a royal holiday in the kingdom, known as *The Day Of Sixty-Nine*. Nobody who wasn't on the inside of royal matters knew exactly what the hell Emperor Nicky meant but he was the sort of jolly king who didn't give a damn. So on that day the country celebrates the number Sixty-Nine without really knowing what all the shouting is about. To most it is the date of a historic battle or the beginning of the dynasty's reign. They've had a lot of Nickies in their time.

Brigitte, emotional as ever, wept for the good old days. But she wept happily, tears being one of her main armaments in the battle against Life and Old Age. That, and of

125

course, her incredible sexual drive. In which case, she was not alone, my friends.

"*Sacré*, Rod . . . you must never leave France. You must never leave Brigitte!"

"Who, me?"

I never argue with great ladies who are great lays.

CHAPTER TEN

Before I began my long series of plans for that important evening, I took Brigitte Lebeau out for a decent meal. She certainly had it coming to her. Apart from her fantastic cooperation on the peace talks assignment, and in the sack, of course, I wanted to blow her to a fine meal.

Like the joke goes, we should have stood in bed.

A lot of *Parisienne* rats were working underground. But how could I know that? There I was, hale and hearty after a splendid joust with Madame Brigitte among her fading percales and the Paris sun was high in the sky. We were hungry, so I promised her a steak, with all the trimmings and all the good cognac she could hold if she would merely pick a place.

She picked the *Salon des Artistes*, a posh eatery along the sidewalks where many a canopy shrouds many an outside table. She said it was merely a ten-block walk and since it was such a lovely new day, why shouldn't we walk, she suggested.

So we walked.

I guess my defenses were down. I was envisioning a fine meal, then packing Brigitte back to her dump on the winding hill and then I would be off to see about my plans for the Hotel Fourchette that night. Walrus-moustache was already busy with his sundry tasks and I was sure the wrap-up would go off as scheduled. I was beginning to miss America.

So there we were, arm-in-arming along the sidewalk, watching the taxicabs scuttle, admiring Paris' boulevards and sights and sounds and smells. Brigitte had wrapped herself in a shawl of sorts and another of the too-tight dresses that showed every rounded line of her packed body. She was happy too. She sang a lot of risque Edith Piaf songs under her breath as we strolled.

And suddenly, out of a clear blue sky, she stopped singing and nudged my arm.

"*Cheri,* we are being followed!"

127

I stopped too, looking back. "Where?"

She wagged her head helplessly.

"I do not know for certain. It is only that I, Brigitte, who have been followed by men all my life, tell you this: somebody is following us!"

"See anything at all?" My questing eyes saw only strollers, men sitting at tables behind newspapers, mademoiselles walking French poodles.

"*Mais non!* But I feel it in my bones, I tell you—"

"I'll take your word for it. Just keep walking as if nothing unusual had happened. I'll keep my eyes peeled."

"I am frightened. Who would follow us? Unless it is the men who did those awful things to Danielle."

"Don't think about that now. Promenade, Madame. You look beautiful."

"Ah, *tres gallant,* Rod!"

Gallant, hooey. She did look like a million dollars and I was still starved. And I didn't want to waltz around with thugs or policemen or any more of the mad crowd from *Les Deuces.* But when you have the sort of fame and reputation I have, anything is possible.

We cut across the avenue at the next interesction, and try as I might, I could find no one and nothing suspicious in the average-looking, customary strollers enjoying the new day. There were a couple of swell-nifty dolls about ten paces behind us but it couldn't have been them. It would have been a crime if it had been them. They were young, full of life and showing every bit of it in mini-skirts and picture hats. I tightened my hold on Brigitte's arm. The streetlight was on red. We waited. Traffic streamed toward us. Cabs, busses, Fiats, Renaults, all kinds of foreign cars. The street was noisy with sound.

The light changed to green and I hustled her over to the far sidewalk. She was out of breath now and her breasts were dancing under her dress. No matter how old she got she would never wear a bra. It was an insult to her.

I was beginning to wish I was carrying another kind of rod. Brigitte had made me jumpy with her fears and ruined the whole day.

Fears?

She was a mind-reader and had eyes in the back of her

128

head. We hadn't gone five steps down the next avenue when it happened. All in a hurry and without even a moment's warning. I had my eyes wide open, but it happened too fast even for a Speedy Gonzales like me.

I had Brigitte's arm anchored in the crook of my own when two guys in striped pants, formal jackets and tall silk hats suddenly were blocking our path. Madame Brigitte squealed in alarm as she threw on the brakes to avoid crashing into them. I stopped dead in my tracks. The two men, looking like refugees from a diplomatic function, both had spade beards, trim moustaches and identically cold eyes. They were also oblivious of all the passersby jostling past us. It showed right out of their cold bleak eyes.

"You will please us greatly if you accompany us, Monsieur Damon."

The one who spoke smiled and did not tip his topper to Brigitte.

"Sorry," I said. "No autographs." I tried to step around him with Brigitte hanging on but his crony blocked me and also opened his mouth.

"I have a gun, Monsieur," this one said. "It is very large and of high caliber. A wound offered at stupidly short range is no challenge. You would be dead before you hit the sidewalk. No, do not scream, Madame. The same bullets would do the same thing to you, I am afraid."

I tightened my grip on her wrist. Both the two top-hatted men couldn't have looked sweeter about the whole thing. We were up against what the hard-boiled detectives and policemen call a pair of real pros. Like killers for hire, out to make a "hit" on a "contract". I tried not to perspire in broad daylight.

"Okay," I said. "What do we do now?"

"We go for a charming ride," the first man said. He waved an arm, indicating a long Daimler parked at the curb. There was no driver visible. "Won't you join us?"

"We insist," the other one said, taking Brigitte by the elbow and escorting her. "To see Paris properly one must truly tour it."

"And leave the driving to you, right?" I gritted, following. No one in our immediate vicinity would have given a

129

second thought to what was going on. Ostensibly, two VIPs were inviting a pair of friends for a ride. In the country or the city, it didn't matter which.

So that's how we got shanghaied in broad daylight and were driven through the streets of Paris toward the open fields beyond the city. I and Brigitte sat in the back of the limousine while the top-hatted duo sat on the front seat. One drove and the other was turned toward us, pointing out the sights with one long ugly pistol with silencer attached. Madame Brigitte Lebeau was for once tongue-tied with fright. Murder and violence and sex and excitement are not compatible bedfellows at all. Damn the Thaddeus X. Coxe Foundation. They *will* get me killed one of these days.

I never did find out the names of our hijackers so I called them Alphonse and Gaston. Alphonse was the one that was driving. Gaston had the gun.

"Who are you?" I asked, trying to look indignant. I *was* indignant. "What the hell are you bothering us for?"

Alphonse chuckled and Gaston brushed a speck of dust off the tip of his silencer-gun.

"You are Rod Damon of America," Gaston purred. "Quite naturally, you are here to see the wonders of the *Académie Sexualité*. Quite undercover, you have put your nose into matters that should not concern you. So what do we do? We remove the nose."

I again tried not to sweat. Brigitte was moaning low.

"What are you talking about? I'm just a tourist, Madame here has been my companion—"

Alphonse gritted out a French oath and Gaston shook his head. The gun pointed at my forehead.

"Please, Monsieur. I beg of you. Treat us as equals. Not as idiots. You have been assigned to protect the Peace Talks conference. We have been assigned to sabotage the Peace Talks conference. It is as simple as that. Now we have you so we will remove you as a threat to our efforts. You see? A matter of simple logic. We cancel you out and our hopes for success mount to the skies. Where shall we kill them, *mon ami?*" He asked Alphonse that the same way you would ask a pal how he likes his eggs? Scrambled or sunny-side up?

Alphonse considered only a second. "There is a small
130

bridge between the villages of Bal and Arlienne. Why not there? It is always deserted and they will sink to the bottom of the lake unseen."

"Good," Gaston purred again. "I'm in favor of that. No one must know what befell these two. At least, not until our plans mature a bit. To the river then. Make all haste."

The Daimler shot down the roadway, kicking up pebbles, dust and all that was left of my nerves. Poor Brigitte was almost in a swoon. It can't be much fun sitting around listening to a pair of clowns discuss how they are going to kill you.

I rallied a mite.

"Who put you up to this? Corbeau?"

They eyed each other and laughed.

"Madame Annette at *Les Deuces?*"

Again, they laughed.

"How about that red-headed dame at the Academy? Lilly de Jussac?"

They both erupted at that, snorting through their noses and Gaston nearly had an internal rupture. Finally, he had the gun straightened out again and laughed right in my face.

"Idiot! Those pawns—*pah!* There are bigger people than they involved. But no matter. What do you care who it is? The information will not warm your last moments to the grave. Come, if you are Christian, say your prayers. The bridge is but another ten minutes or so—"

Brigitte Lebeau had gotten some of her wind back.

"Animals," she hissed, shaking. "With a beautiful woman, this is all you can think of?"

Gaston elevated his eyebrows. "Madame?" He didn't quite get her, but I did.

She sneered at him and immediately fumbled for her bosom, which already had enough *décolletage* showing to shame the Seven Hills of Rome. Gaston's eyes suddenly twitched. A full giveaway. He got the picture. And Madame Brigitte Lebeau was no dummy. She was smart. As masterfully smart as she had to be. She had something to sell to save her life. I waited, knowing what she was up to. Alphonse at the wheel was sneaking furtive looks into the rearview mirror. Frenchmen. You can count on them every time. Madame Brigitte was banking on that.

131

"Fool," Brigitte shot out scornfully, 'you would kill a woman like me before making love to her? Prayer? I want nothing from *le bon dieux* but one good roll in the hay before I am to die. What do you say to that, my fine assassin?"

"Madame," Gaston murmured as her fingers kept busy, divesting herself of the upper half of her dress. "Please—this is most—"

"What would you?" she barked. "If you will not service me then let the man here do it. Damon is a giant among men and it would be very shameful of you not to let me taste him once more before there is nothing left of me to love."

Alphonse giggled nervously at the wheel. Gaston flung him a look. A question lurked beneath his fancy eyebrows. Brigitte saw the hesitation and capitalized on it.

"Oh—" She batted her eyelashes. "I would like to have all three of you but if I can only have one, let me at least make love to my lover, Damon. You may watch. We will not run away. At least, you will learn the fine art of love-making. How a woman *should* be loved!"

"Be a sport," I challenged. "What have you got to lose except a little time? So you kill us a half hour later. Big deal."

"Be still," Gaston commanded, his eyes roving over Brigitte's full and glorious mammaries. "The offer is tempting. I am a Frenchman, Madame. To us *l'amour* is all. True. I should be honored to serve you. God knows we deplore the necessity of shooting you. One so lovely—" He inclined his head toward Alphonse. "Pull over to the next convenient copse of woods you see. It seems this assignment has taken on curiously pleasing overtones."

He meant *undertones,* and Alphonse obeyed him with such speed there was no doubt in my mind how he felt about the whole thing. The Daimler jumped, swerved, found a nearby trysting spot. A lover's lane probably, where the milkmaids and the farmhands whooped it up at all hours. It was dense, thickly packed with spruce and birch trees and couldn't be seen at all from the roadway. Madame Brigitte Lebeau was undressed already, save for her shoes. The tight dress was curled down around her

132

shapely ankles. I didn't look at her, though. I knew what she looked like. I was watching Gaston and the gun and hoping that the one he *always* carried was taking his mind off the general situation. I was gambling and so was Brigitte, but what did we have to lose?

"Ah," Brigitte poured it on in her honeyed, bedroom *patois*, "this is so good of you, my friend. I will allow you to drink your fill of my breasts. See them? Are they not round and beautiful?" She practically held them up for Gaston's inspection and Alphonse, who was backing the Daimler carefully within the cozy environs of the trees, lost his bearings and ran smack into a hidden birch that was thicker across the middle than death and taxes.

"*Merde!*" Gastron shrilled. The gun jumped.

"*Rod!*" Madame Brigitte Lebeau screamed like a banshee and kicked one shapely gam up at Gaston's extended pistol.

"*Yippee!*" I chortled and shot forward from the back seat like a battering ram. I didn't stay in shape only for the bedroom ballets. My old college days stand me in good stead and I stay fit and trim. There is a decided relationship between Sex and Calisthenics. A trained body helps in both arenas of accomplishment.

Brigitte's accurate toe sent the gun flying. Gaston cursed and scrambled forward which put his trim jaw closer to my fist. I slammed a five-fingered destroyer at him. A real hard smash. It was a good one. He went flying back, against the door of the car and his body must have hit the handle. The door fell open and he fell out. A tangle of striped pants, morning coat and top hat. By that time, Brigitte was opening her door and flouncing nakedly after him. I forgot about them both and concentrated on Alphonse. What a surprise.

He was coming up with two guns, one in each fist and was really serious about making Swiss cheese out of my face. I ducked just in time. The guns boomed together and chunks of Daimler bounced all around the tonneau. Before he could sight in on me again, I was over the car seat and all over him. He was tall and thin and hard-muscled. I had my hands full. Within seconds, we were asprawl in the roadway, whaling the hell out of each other. He had hung

133

onto the guns, though. Try as I wanted to, I couldn't get him to release them. So I did the next worse thing. I jumped on him with both feet and his eyeballs rolled and the guns went off again. He screamed just once and then rolled over as quiet as a mouse. A backfire, gun turned in on himself, had caught him a bad one dead-center in the heart.

Birds were racing out of the treetops, squawking like crazy, when I ran around to see how Brigitte was making out.

I should have known.

She and Gaston were locked in a fast embrace. Alphonse's friend had his lips mashed to Brigitte's splendid shelf of breast while her left hand was toying with his private weapon. No wonder Gaston had licked his lips at what Brigitte had offered earlier. He had nothing to be ashamed of. Almost a rival for the *Les Deuces* stud, Fountainbleau. But Brigite wasn't as nuts as that sounded. She had the fallen silencer pistol in her right hand, pressing the nose of the thing right against Gaston's left temple.

"Come on," I growled. "No time for that. Get off him, Brigitte. We have to ask him a lot of questions."

"Please, Monsieur," Gaston mumbled, his eyes trying to find me from beneath the harvest of her goodies. "Do me the courtesy of letting me enjoy the same arrangement I was to give you before you died . . ."

"It is only fair, Rod," Brigitte panted, eyes shining. "Yes, this one is not so bad . . ." What a woman.

"Up," I demanded. "And now. There's no time to lose. Come on. Later on you two can tango to your heart's desire."

Frustrated and dissatisfied, they broke apart. Brigitte rolled to her feet, brushing her bared gleaming flesh free of leaves, brambles and dust. Gaston straightened, looking about for his tall top hat. It lay crushed in the bushes, not too far off.

"Never mind your hat, Gaston. Talk." I had taken the gun from Brigitte to level at him. "Who sent you to kill us?"

He shrugged.

"I am an assassin, Monsieur. I never see the people who hire me. It is the arrangement and a good one all around.

134

They have nothing to fear from me and I have nothing to fear from them."

I frowned. "Who gives you these assignments?"

He stiffened, not unproudly. "I have a reputation in the proper circles. I get a call on the phone from a contact. The contact is the one who makes the arrangement with the buyer of my services."

"And who is your contact?"

"Monsieur—please. I cannot tell you. It is our code. And even my contact would not know. These things are planned by so many, what you call middlemen, no one would ever trace the monster back to its source. As it is with a snake with many heads."

"Yeah," I said sourly. "Well, tuck that snake back in your pants. I'm turning you over to the French police."

"As you will." He bowed toward Brigitte Lebeau. "In a way, I am not sorry I have failed."

She glowed like a teenager with her first kiss. Her cheeks flamed red. She made a kissing motion with her lips.

"You see, Rod. A French gentleman. There is nothing finer under God's sky."

"I'll bet. Now, if you don't mind—"

What happened then was one of those things that literally comes like a bolt out of the blue. Blue, hell. It was another of those planned, awful things that assassins and assassin-hirers go in for. Monsieur Gaston didn't have a chance.

He was never going to taste the full fruits of Madame Brigitte Lebeau's garden of goodies.

A rifle shot, long, high and keening, came down out of the hills somewhere and Gaston coughed. Just once. When he stopped coughing, he had pitched forward on his face, full-length down to the ground. Brigitte cried out, hiding her face in her hands before she got enough sense to run screaming to hide in the thickets. I jumped under the stalled Daimler and made myself scarce. The rifle didn't fire again. I think the hidden marksman had accomplished what he had come for.

Gaston was deader than the ten-cent bus ride in the United States. He didn't bat an eye or move a muscle where he lay on the hot, dry earth. A bullet had found his vital organs just as one had put his partner Alphonse out of business.

The French vaudeville act was dead. And whoever had hired the two Frenchies to put Rod Damon out of action had sent along a spare gun to make sure that everything turned out okay. Maybe to kill the assassins too after they killed us—to really nail down the lid of secrecy on the whole affair. Peace Talks, hah. It was a real old-fashioned shooting war.

"Brigitte," I called. "Get into the car. We're getting the hell out of here."

"I'm afraid!" It was a whimper of sound from the brush.

"Coast is clear. See . . . ?" I scampered out from beneath the Daimler and got in behind the wheel. It was not my plan to lug two dead bodies back to town. They could stay out here and rot for all I cared.

Brigitte finally found enough nerve to come pell-mell out of the brush like a naked Diana and barrel for the car. She hurtled in beside me and huddled against me. I waited a long moment while she got her hysteria under control. What a dame! She went from wails of fear to moans of ecstasy in a flick of her false eyelashes.

"Oh, *cherie* . . ."

"Now what's bothering you? You were a brave girl. Offering yourself that way so we could get out of that sticky situation. So why are you coming apart at the seams now?"

"It's all this killing," she wailed. "*Sacré!* So many corpses. All for the Peace? Pah! And what will happen tonight at your grand affair at the Fourchette?"

"That remains to be seen. Get some clothes on. We're going back to town."

"Must we?"

"We must."

Her ever-curious fingers were playing around my crotch, trying to unearth the old truths about me. Her breath had quickened and a lazy look was lidding her eyes.

"Very nice . . . may I? . . . only a moment . . . and then we can ride from this scene of carnage. . . ."

"Brigitte, you are absolutely insatiable!"

"Isn't that nice?"

136

"Well—what the hell—be my guest." Feebly, I sat back against the cushioned Daimler seat and relaxed. It was time to do some more thinking before I got my show on the road. The two new corpses and the murder attempt had made me see the coming party in a new and more terrible light. It wasn't going to be all fun and games. It couldn't be, not when somebody cares enough to send the very best assassins to murder you. And you can quote me.

The birds were back, humming and tweeting. Brigitte Lebeau had wangled one of her creamy incredible thighs over my lap so that all I had to do was angle a bit and the Gods of love could be served once more. What the hell. Life is for the living and I knew that Alphonse and Gaston would have changed places with me in five seconds flat if I had asked them.

So I angled and let Brigitte enjoy the sheathing of the greatest thing I have. She caught her breath and her eyeballs rolled again and her nipples hardened and we were off and running.

"Rod!" she gasped. "At the first entry, it is always like the first time. So new, so exciting . . . so wonderful!"

"You like me, huh?"

"Like? That is not the word. I am—how you say—nuts for you, baby."

"Nuts it is, then. I'm not exactly sensible about you either."

So once more we locked horns in that equal struggle we shared. My brain filed away the Daimler's front seat as pleasurable, roomy enough and quite more satisfactory than Cadillacs, Fords, Plymouths or Buicks as a rolling motel to ball in.

But all the time my mind alas, strayed to the coming event of the evening. The Hotel Fourchette and my planned party. A big affair to trap the people responsible for Danielle Lebeau's murder and all the skullduggery that was holding up the Peace Talks in Paris.

What a whacky life it truly is.

The fate of the world was resting in the hands of a man who felt that making love to women is all that *everything* is about.

Not the world I made, see?

Let's keep the record straight.

137

"Rod . . . ?"

"Mmmmmmmmm?"

"Do you think my daughter's murderer will come to the Hotel Fourchette tonight?"

"Brigitte, my darling . . ."

"Yes, my Rod?"

"Less talk, more action."

She never did get the steak I promised her. But I didn't leave her hungry. . . .

CHAPTER ELEVEN

The very important party held on the third floor of the Hotel Fourchette might have gone down in French history except for a few necessary particulars. It was a top secret affair but by the time it had endings that justified all my means, quite a few rugs were kicked back, many a chandelier was swung from and more than one private gong was kicked to hell and around. But more of that anon.

Firstly, let me say that my walrus-moustached miracle worker was just that. The sound camera equipment cleverly concealed on all the walls and apertures of every room on the floor was an engineering feat worthy of Frank Lloyd Wright. Also, he had rounded up a sleepy-eyed little French camera genius named René Rolfe who was some kind of big deal with the Gallic cinema people and had won a flock of awards and badges for his highly documentary films. This ace I planted in a wall closet niche in the main room that my plan needed. The niche was covered with a thick tapestry studded into place with rhinestones. But there were openings between the studs and the wall and Monsieur Rolfe had a nifty camera with zoom lens and a thousand other niceties of modern photography. Before the guests came I gave him his instructions. He spoke English. With an accent like Louis Jordan.

"You know what you have to do, Monsieur Rolfe. I want everything. Don't shrink from ugliness or the truth. This is for France!"

His cigarette was almost larger than he was. His pullover cap wider than his shoulders. He fit into the wall space like a piece of furniture.

"Monsieur Damon," he sniffed. "I shot fifty miles of film for *le documentaire* known as *The Sewers of Paris*. What can you show me I have not seen?"

"Pardon, but this will be all about sex. It's—rather different, don't you think?"

He chuckled and poked his cigarette at me. "Not as

139

much as all that. Show me your worst. I, René Rolfe, will film it."

"You're on your own. Stay out of sight no matter what you see and no matter what happens, keep grinding away."

I closed the tapestry over his smiling face and went to the main door to greet my guests as they came on the scene. I was happy with my arrangement. The room was large, with enough divans, lounges and stuffed chairs to accommodate the chorus of the *Folies Bergeres*. The far wall held a twenty-by-twenty-foot movie screen, already in place, and the movie projector I had acquired through Walrus-moustache's good work was already set up against the back wall on the big marble coffee table. I had held one thing back from my employer. When I was through with Brigitte Lebeau for the afternoon, I had driven to the Left Bank in the Renault and made a considerable dent in my expense money by buying several juicy reels of the lewdest and most torrid stag movie film I could find. The Black Market had charged me an arm and a leg, but it was all part of my plan.

I personally had mixed batches of martinis, gimlets and whiskey sours in three huge vats of the sauce, carefully spiking it liberally with the LSD which Walrus-moustache had grudgingly provided through the services of a local hospital eager to cooperate with the American government. Walrus-moustache would not be at the party, but on the floor above, carefully taking pictures of his own, along with tape recording equipment, to memorialize the occasion for his own files at the Coxe Foundation. The stage was indeed set. The party was ready. All I needed was the cast of characters. I kept my fingers crossed, hoping I had not misjudged Madame Annette and her weirdo playmate, Wan Lo. Time would tell.

A few minutes after the stroke of the hour, they began to arrive. I wasn't expecting Brigitte Lebeau, as I had other plans for her.

Like all schoolgirls the world over, Mady Morrow and Viviane Fresnay were the first to show up. Punctuality was a habit with them already. They looked good enough to eat. Mady had poured her ample, curvy dimensions into an abbreviated cocktail frock of blue, while the more sophisticated, more classic Viviane was unforgettable

140

dynamite in a pale orange thing that barely covered her body. In the blonde and brunette class, they were a pair of winners. *Aces.*

We kissed all around and I gave them some good advice.

"Listen. You must promise me. Don't touch any of the hard liquor in this place except the champagne over there in the buckets." When they made faces at that, I explained how I had drugged the rest of the hootch. Their eyes widened and they both giggled. Mady patted my best resting place.

"You for real?" Mady Morrow asked. "What kind of party is this?"

"I'm trapping Danielle Lebeau's murderer and doing my damnedest to help the peace talks. That a good enough reason?"

Viviane shivered. "For that we will do anything. Not even taste hard liquor. Besides, who can argue when there is champagne?"

"Right," Mady said breezily. "I kind of hinted to Madame, Rod. You can expect her with a couple of the girls from the Academy. Her kind of girls. I said you had made it kind of a come one, come all party."

"Good girl. Look, both of you go nibble on some champagne corks. I want to be at the door when they come in." They nodded, drifting off in clouds of loveliness. I expected them both to be a big help. The largest part of what was coming had to be Madame Annette and her *Les Deuces* crowd, plus the extra special guests I wanted. Without them, the whole idea would be a big bust.

She didn't disappoint me, because about eleven forty-five, she came sweeping through the door in a fur-trimmed ermine dress that swept the floor as she came. With her was Wan Lo, radiant in loose-fitting mandarin jacket and pantaloons plus slippers. Behind them, Françoise Marnay and Mei Ling High entered arm-in-arm. They were bearing up nobly under the weight of enormous baubles, bangles and beads. Like love people. I had to shake hands with the bronze stud, choked to death in tie and tails, all harnessed up and sulky. Michel-Duval Fountainbleau himself. He couldn't resist grabbing my shipping department as he walked by me so I kicked him in the fanny just to show him there were no hard feelings. And as the minutes ticked away, I hit the jackpot.

In marched Gaston Corbeau. Short, fat, his ambassadorial sash gleaming red and with him came the Viet Nam and Viet Cong characters I so desperately wanted to see. I couldn't pronounce their names but I didn't have to. Madame Annette came sweeping back, both hands holding cocktail glasses brimming with gin and everything was going according to plan.

"Rod, dear man, this is Monsieur Corbeau of the French government and these are two of my dearest friends from Asia." She rattled off their names and they bowed, smiling. Two undersized little men, with lots of things on their minds besides peace talks. Right after that, a lady ambassador showed up. A tall, big-chested dowager type in steel harness and jewels, looking down her nose at me. Madame Kingston from the United Kingdom, Aussie style. She too it seemed was one of the gay beautiful crowd that loved what went on at *Les Deuces*. She was built like a steamrollered bra.

And then Madame Lilly de Jussac showed up and promptly stole the show. What waste it was. When a girl with a towering pile of flaming red hair and smoldering breasts, hips and eyes, pours it all into a sleek evening gown and then pours it all down the drain by being a Lesbian, what can you do but weep for mankind?

On each of her arms were two slender, willowly branched-out busty young damsels from the *Académie Sexualité*. The Mlles. Risseur and Blondelle. A pip of a pair and just the kind of ammunition needed for my plan. Both of them had lips like swabs.

"Coward," Madame Lilly hissed as I led her into the heart of the room. "Why did you not tell me of this party today when we met? I had to learn of it from Morrow!"

"I like surprises."

"And tomorrow? You will keep your promise about my challenge at *Les Deuces?*"

"There is no tomorrow," I whispered like Charles Boyer. "Only tonight. Have a drink? Gimlet, martini, whiskey sour? Champagne?"

"Martini. I prefer gin to sweet drinks."

142

"You would. Hang onto your playmates and I'll be right back."

Before I could get back, Madame Annette collared me and drew Gaston Corbeau and the Asian big wheels into a cross-fire conversation about sex, love and the peace talks. Wan Lo hung back, beaming. He was in his glory. The bronze stud, a bodyguard type all the way, wasn't too far from Annette's elbow. Things were going fine, though. Viviane Fresnay and Mady Morrow, highly decorative, were walking about the big room, admiring things, acting like a pair of lovelies with all the time in the world on their hands. Françoise Marnay and Mei Ling High ignored everybody else. Including me. They only had eyes for each other. The best part of it, though, was everybody was sampling all the spiked stuff. I only heard one champagne cork explode before I got around to showing my stag movies.

But not before a lot more weirdos in odd clothes and long hair, so you couldn't tell the boys from the girls, showed up, courtesy Madame Annette and her *Les Deuces*. They all wore billowing clothes and I wondered if these weren't Annette's secret cameramen who were to grind away when the party got more interesting. I was sure she was going to convert my party to her own rotten ends. But I was going to beat her to the punch.

Thanks to the LSD in the drinks and the cooperation of Walrus-moustache, René Rolfe and my two little *agents provocatrices*, Mady Morrow and Viviane Fresnay.

I waited until about twelve thirty when some of my famous guests began to reel, until Gaston Corbeau had decided that Viviane Fresnay was just the girl for him, and the two Oriental advisers were squabbling over the merits of Mady Morrow, one on each arm and pulling away.

"Ladies and gentlemen," I called. "Everybody take a seat, will you please? You are about to see a movie I made a long time ago. I promise you will not be bored. It's rather a distinctive film."

The guests all laughed and clapped their hands. Unless I was crazy, it didn't look like the LSD had worked its magic madness yet. But you can never tell. It sneaks up on you, from what trip-takers say.

143

So everybody began to flop down in various parts of the room, facing the white screen on the far wall. I walked to the projector, adjusted it and asked Mei Ling High to hit the wall switch. She favored me with a toothy smile, because she was busy nibbling on Françoise Marnay's right shoulder. So Wan Lo obliged, skipping to the wall like the proper elf he was and blowing me a kiss across his pudgy fingertips. Oh, how I wanted to kick his mincing ass all around the room. But I had bigger game to bag.

The big room went dark, the projector lit up and I hit the FORWARD switch. At long last, the show was really on the road.

My show.

The one that was calculated to save the world for peace talks. And rid the conference of the big threat of Red Chinese nuclear chop suey.

I hoped.

It was a charming little film. Charming by all heterosexual standards. Not a work of art, surely nothing for an Oscar or even the Late Late Show. But it was all it had to be and more. A raw, unabashed, free-swinging sex movie whose plot and cast of characters were also no more than they had to be. The star had all the requirements. A twelve-inch slab of swinging, sizzling meat and a willingness to take on all the sex-hungry broads in the picture. Which meant one blonde, one redhead and one brunette outrageously built, beyond the realm of belief, posing as farmer's daughters out to please the city slicker whose car broke down beside the meadow where they were supposed to be sunbathing in the lake. Pretty soon, sunbathing was the last thing the picture was about. The movie hero was the Eighth Wonder of the Man World. What he did to those three broads during one half hour of smoking film would have set an asbestos curtain on fire. What it did to my houseguests more than compensated.

In the dark, I heard giggles, then moans, then those harsh intakes of breath which clearly tell how much the breather has been impressed. Cocktail glasses tinkled. Somebody yelled out: *"Ooolala!"* followed by a chorus of Bravos, Magnifiques and Encores!

It was, very obviously, their kind of cinema.

The dirty film, and the dirty LSD, were combining to do their very nice piece of dirty work. When I slipped another film into the projector, without turning up the lights, the damage was already being done. Somebody was on the floor next to the projector, trying to pull my pants down. It was Wan Lo. "Oh, please," he whimpered in a girlish voice. "Nobody will see. . . ."

I wondered what Monsieur René Rolfe the great cinematographer thought of the smoker film from his wall niche behind the tapestry. Or was he working up a sweat too?

Wan Lo started to tug on me in earnest. I did him a great favor. I slugged him, smack on the mouth and he went down, laughing merrily. I was beginning to sweat myself. All around us in the darkness, the craziest medley of noises and sounds could be heard. I took a chance. Maybe the time I wanted was right now. I batted the projector lever to STOP, found the wall switch and turned on the lights.

Again, I had hit the jackpot. A double jackpot.

In the flood of exposure, the room was chaos. Not so much sex as a roomful of drugged, worn-out specimens that once were people. Only Viviane Fresnay and Mady Morrow were on their feet. They gawked along with me at the spectacle of the room. It was a mess.

The LSD had hit them hard, all of them. They were flying, reeling, staggering, slobbering. Françoise Marnay and Mei Ling High, for whom no one else was alive, had their skirts pulled high and were going at it like it was their last chance on earth. Madame Annette was tearing her fur-trimmed dress off, babbling incoherently for a whipping. The weird assortment of gays and girls from her club were rolling on the floor, rolling and moaning. And poor dear Madame Lilly de Jussac had both her escorts where she wanted them. Twirling their hairdos and panting like puppies as they scampered around her naked thighs. For a long merry moment, the tableau held like something in a stop-action motion picture still. Andy Warhol, hooey. This was a little bit of Olson and Johnson, a lot of Marx Brothers madness and a ton of perversion in action.

Michel-Duval Fountainbleau, his eyes two flaming balls of bull fever, was riding his broomstick around the big room, yelling like a Comanche, trying to stab anything in sight that was open. Bare-assed broads parted before him like the sea did for Moses. The whooping, whomping gays from *Les Deuces* transformed into a horde of simpering maniacs, begging for some stud power. I saw Fountainbleau go down to the floor, taking about a half-dozen fans with him. Fans of both sexes.

The Vietcong and Viet Nam diplomats were ringing around the rosie with Madame Kingston and that gallant old girl was doing her best to show them what the Open Door policy really meant. In a trice, the three of them were tearing at each other in a frenzy or arms, legs and tongues.

Madame Annette had gotten down to the buff and was battering and ramming herself away at a tall statue of Adonis in one corner of the room who she must have thought was Michel-Duval Fountainbleau. Poor whore.

Ouch.

My dear Madame Lilly de Jussac was in the French version of Seventh Heaven. Her two acolytes were in flames now. Slavering away on the floor at her feet, both trying to get their mouths into working position. The Madame had a sappy grin on her face and her mouth was forming obscene words. Risseur and Blondelle were foaming.

As for Gaston Corbeau and the Orientals, all of them had the same idea. They were chasing poor Madame Kingston all around the sofas and chairs, hands on their tools, ready to use them. There was no time to lose. I signaled to Viviane and Mady and we went into action like a team. Michel-Duval Fountainbleau came up from the floor, bolting for me, so I kicked him again. Down he went and before he could gather himself together, I and my two helpers had quickly, firmly, guided Corbeau and the men of South East Asia and Madame Kingston out of the horn parlor. The leering men came because Viviane and Mady showed them some skin and promised all sorts of pleasures in low, lilting voices. Within a quick minute, we were outside the suite and the plan was working without a hitch. I took a leather billy out of my back pocket and put the slug on all of the VIPs. They went down without a murmur and fell asleep on the tiled floor of the room. Again I clapped my hands and Viviane and

Mady had no idea what was coming next. How could they?

From the next room, summoned by my signal, trooped a veritable horde of prostitutes. Veterans of the foreign wars. I had recruited that afternoon a dozen of the hoariest, henna-haired whores who roamed the Paris streets. They too would work for France, but the one hundred bucks I gave each of them and their own natural desires would take care of the rest. I had picked aceys and acey-deuceys.

"Remember!" I shouted, pushing the dirty dozen into the room. *"Pour la belle France!"*

Giggling, shrieking, pawing like so many alleycats they spilled into the room. I slammed the doors shut and double-bolted them. I leaned against the barrier and waited. I didn't mop my face with a handkerchief until the great war cry went up and from behind the doors came literal frenzy of cries, yells and screams as each of the ladies of the evening picked out a sex partner.

"And now, René Rolfe," I said with a prayer. "Do your stuff."

Mady Morrow and Viviane Fresnay exchanged glances. I was grateful to them for their help and later I would show them how grateful. But not just yet. We still had work to do. Though the worst of it was over.

"What's going on in there, Rod?" Mady Morrow said sullenly. "It sounds like a lot of fun."

"Yes," Viviane tittered. "Even Madame will not be safe."

"Don't you believe it," I said. "It's the sort of ball when put on highly directed and edited film that will make all those worms in there crawl back into the ground and stop messing up the peace talks."

Mady laughed and crouched at the keyholes. She didn't come up for air for a full two minutes. She looked dazed. The shouting had loudened.

"And my mother used to wallop me for sucking my thumb. Take a look, Viviane. You won't believe what the Madame is up to."

Viviane looked. When she turned away, she crossed herself.

"She has reached the very limit. I wouldn't believe it if I
147

hadn't seen it with my own eyes."

I rubbed my hands. If René Rolfe was all he said he was, we would have a lulu of a film. A hit picture. A very hit picture.

"You girls can go home now. I promise I'll be along in an hour or two. I want to wrap this up. If it's okay with you, we can *ménage à trois*."

"Why leave the building?" Mady asked. "Where's *your* room?"

"Yes," Viviane said in a dreamy voice. "I think I would like that too. The film was rather—ah—stimulating."

I knew what she meant, but Brigitte Lebeau was in my room. At the last second, I had put a sleeping pill in her coffee because I'd been afraid she'd louse things up by going for Madame Lilly de Jussac like a lovesick cow. I had wanted no interference.

"Ah—okay. What the hell. Room Seven. Just down the hall. Dany's mother is in there, but you three can kind of talk it over, huh? Now, please beat it."

From behind the locked doors, tigerish, unearthly growls and moans emanated. Mady Morrow and Viviane Fresnay delayed no longer. "You hurry!" they chimed in unison and raced out of the room. They left in a flurry of skirts and bared legs. They smelled nice too.

Ten minutes later, Walrus-moustache entered from the hallway, his face drawn and bloodless. He actually staggered toward me, gasping.

"S'matter?" I said. "Can't take any more?"

"Good God, Damon, I have all the material we'll ever need. What a carnal outrage. Shocking! Absolutely inhuman. That LSD is pure poison."

"You bet it is. But it worked. Never knock a successful formula." He kept shaking his head, dumbfounded by life in the raw.

Another five minutes passed and the sounds from within had abated. Some furniture had made noise crashing around but now a deathly silence ensued. I looked at my watch and decided it was time.

I opened the doors and René Rolfe fell into my arms. He was as white as a sheet, rolls of film in their cans dangling from his scrawny neck. I caught him in my arms and he nodded in gratitude. An unlit lipburner was stuck in one corner of his mouth, long since gone out. I was surprised he hadn't swallowed it.

"Rolfe, you okay—?"

"Monsieur . . ." His eyes batted weakly. "I want my wife . . . my wife!"

"The film," I snarled. "Did you take the pictures?"

"Film! Mother of the saints—*diabolique!*—never have I seen such carnality. I weep for mankind . . . but I must hurry home to see my wife Eloise . . . *ma chere* Eloise!"

We let him go but not before I had about three cans of five hundred feet each of the most explosive footage in the history of France. Maybe the world.

Walrus-moustache took one last peek through the keyhole. He straightened, shuddering and took the cans of film from me.

"*Fin,*" he murmured. "They all look like they're sleeping now. What a chaos . . ."

"Good. Now all you have to do is return these four sleeping diplomats to their respective hotels without any more nonsense and then I'll personally supervise the editing of this film and tomorrow I want you to pull another string. Arrange and set up an embassy luncheon where we can show these pictures. The difference is that we can privately shame these people into taking off and going into hiding where they won't bother the peace talks anymore. People like Corbeau, Madame Kingston and these two Southeast Asians don't do their countries, and the world, one lick of good."

"Check, Damon." He sighed again and stared at the supine ambassadors dozing on the floor. "Fools all of them. If only they'd do these intrigues and affairs of theirs with a little *élan.*"

"What you really mean is—keep it to themselves."

"Check."

He'd never know how much I agreed with him on that particular point. Sex should always be a pretty private affair.

At least, with not more than four people involved.

Which reminded me of Brigitte Lebeau, Mady Morrow and Viviane Fresnay and Room Seven. My room. I was tired. Dead-tired now. I did need some sleep, after all. The night and its tensions had worn me. The Hotel Fourchette floor plan had called for a lot of maneuvering to make sure everything went off without a hitch.

I said goodnight to Walrus-moustache and went down the hall to my room. Let the shamed-faces in the movie room sleep off their LSD nightmares. I didn't care if all of them committed suicide and took a dive out of the hotel window. One of them was Danielle Lebeau's actual murderer and all of them were as guilty as hell in my book.

In my room, the light was out and there was a rustle of movement on the double-bed. I lurched toward it, undoing my tie.

"Ah, it is he at last," Brigitte Lebeau chuckled in the darkness. "The good, kind, oh so generous Monsieur Rod Damon."

"Yes." That was Viviane Fresnay's dreamy little whisper. "He is a boon to all womankind."

I sat down on the edge of the bed and immediately, three pairs of feminine arms engulfed me with caresses, tugs and pulls.

My wheel of fortune spun merrily for a time. Oh, it was a helluva thing. To be incorporated like that with three revolving partners of such solid, unquestionable assets. The mutual firm of Lebeau, Morrow and Fresnay were so very anxious to pour all their holdings into the Damon Foundation. For once I had my own Thaddeaus X. Coxe thing. My own little harvest of goodies, with me calling all the shots. *Merveilleux,* as they say on the Left Bank and in all good bedrooms everywhere.

Brigitte cooed in my left ear, Mady busied herself with the family jewels and that delightful little minx, Viviane, found a surprise down among my sheltering palms.

It was so easy and relaxing to forget the whole fandango of the peace talks and the mission to Paris which had brought these sexy delights into my arms. The hotel room was a bower of peace and plenty. It is my only platform, my only plank, for true Peace. If the world made more love, we wouldn't have anything ever like Vietnam or the coming Third World War.

My kind of Coming is my answer for everything.

My plank will withstand any kind of pressure or scrutiny or examination. Ask my three little maids of whoopee.

150

"You—" Brigitte panted.

"Are—" Mady whispered.

"The Greatest!" Viviane exploded, departing from her sheer French expressiveness.

I do not come by my Ego easily. It is built on a solid record of success. Walrus-moustache is right. I am the greatest Coxeman of them all. For I have roamed nobly on behalf of the world's security.

And Brigitte Lebeau wasn't mad at me for slipping her a Mickey Finn and Viviane Fresnay was still weary of the female tongue and Mady Morrow still preferred hers straight.

So we had another party.

With one walloping difference.

Nobody was taking any pictures.

If they had, I would have crowned them.

As I happily lunged away at my work, I thought of tomorrow and the grand surprise I had planned for the embassy luncheon. As well as my last tournament with Madame Lilly de Jussac.

The poor dame didn't know it but she had licked her last lollipop at the *Académie Sexualité*.

There was going to be a new order of things.

The world dances on . . . and what goes up must come down, and vice versa.

"Now me," said Brigitte Lebeau.

"No, me," said Viviane Fresnay.

"Me!" said Mady Morrow.

Yes, sir, it was a mad old pinwheel that last night in the Hotel Fourchette. I must admit I had a *forking* good time.

We went around and around in circles.

151

CHAPTER TWELVE

Well, that about wraps up the Paris Affair. Or affairs. If you prefer precise nomenclature.

We ran the film at the Embassy Luncheon the next day. When René Rolfe finally could be dragged out of his wife Eloise's arms, he ruefully edited and looped the film for me. He had outdone himself. The man was a genius. Imagine fifteen hundred feet of the tightest shots, real close-ups, artistic compositions of all sorts of faces, legs, navels and choicer portions of the male and female anatomy. What made the film particularly effective was that the LSD had confused everybody to hell. The normals and the naturals had mixed it up like mad so that boys were doing it to boys, thinking they were girls and in reverse confusion. Rolfe's footage was as sharp and clear as if he had used natural light. Annette, Wan Lo, the stud, Madame de Jussac, Françoise Marnay and Mei Ling High were all seen having their jollies in the lewdest, most explicit ways. Of course, Madame Kingston, Gaston Corbeau and the Southeast Asians were in the film too even if not involved in the actual obscene footage but Rolfe had lensed them chasing around the room, making fools of themselves over Viviane Fresnay and Mady Morrow and that was good enough to discredit them. I only had to show about twenty minutes of the film before a French dignitary bellowed for me to turn the projector off and then soundly and roundly denounced the guilty ambassadors. When they slunk out of the room, they were going home in disgrace, to be rapidly replaced by the sort of men who wouldn't have their heads turned by a piece of tail. Madame Annette, of course, and her weird sadomasochistic *Les Deuces*, was raided that very day and put out of business. Walrus-moustache produced the murder weapon which had killed Danielle Lebeau and the French police had no trouble beating a confession out of Wan Lo. He loved every minute of the third degree, naturally. With the plot exposed, the sabotage plan was a dead dirty bird.

So the peace talks resumed without fuss or muss, and

the world and the newspapers never really knew how close they came to being scuttled for all time. The Red Chinese dummied up and said no more.

When Walrus-moustache and I were on the steps of the embassy building, his eyes shone with admiration.

"My boy, I'm proud of you. You've covered the Coxe Foundation with glory once again."

"How proud?"

He smiled as if he had an ace up his sleeve. As it turned out, he did.

"Proud enough to grant you an indefinite leave of absence from the Foundation. Stay in Paris, enjoy yourself. In fact"—his eyes twinkled—"how would you like to be the new head of the *Académie Sexualité?*"

I thought of all those leather mini-skirts, those white middie blouses and lost my head. I took the job. I thanked him warmly and he handed me one of the cans of hot film.

"Here. Take this with you and go see Madame Lilly de Jussac. And kick her out on her elegant rear end. She's through, as of now. The Foundation cabled me this morning. The job is yours if you want it."

"Temporarily, it sounds like fun. Thanks."

"Forget it. I'll see you—eventually."

He waved goodbye and I bounced down the stone steps of the embassy building and vaulted into the Renault. Paris smiled that day.

I think I broke every speed limit in Paris, racing for the *Académie Sexualité.*

And those hundreds of sexy, swinging young things that yearned to know what little boys were made of. Well, I was just the stud to show them and tell them and lead them out of the wilderness of their naivete and ignorance.

Madame Lilly de Jussac was already packing. Stuffing some papers and notes into a leather briefcase in her *sanctum sanctorum* as I bowled my way in. She was dressed in the leather regulation skirt and she still was going topless. I wondered if she was going to leave the building that way. The Hong Kong Flu just never seemed to bother that bonnie broad.

I dropped the can of hot film on her desk.

"What's your hurry? Got a woman waiting for you?"

She stiffened as if I had insulted her. A fine flush of red filled her cheeks. All four of them.

"You have won. I am disgraced. I can teach these young ladies no more. Do with them what you will. I know you are replacing me. The building has buzzed with comment all morning."

Three ways not to keep a secret: telephone, telegraph, tell a woman. I bet Walrus-moustache had told Brigitte Lebeau earlier that day when they were shacked up at her place and the redoubtable ex-Fifi La Fleur had passed the word on to Mady Morrow and Viviane Fresnay. Dames. How can you beat them?

"You can't go, Lilly," I said. "Oh, you're fired and all that and I do plan some excellent symposiums all the rest of the week. But you can't go."

She stopped packing and drew herself up proudly. *Mamma mia*, what a fine figure of a woman she was!

"And why not, may I ask? What's to keep me here?"

"I want you to stay and take lessons from me. You can be saved, you know."

"Really? What is it you want of me? Another feather for your oh so protean cap?" She deliberately avoided the can of film.

"Uh uh," I said, putting my arms around her and taking each of her incredible breasts full in the face. "I have to find out whether you're a real redhead or not."

"Is that all that interests you?" she sighed wearily, letting herself sag against me. She began to cry softly. I kissed the yummy tips of her areolas. She shuddered and held me tight, her fantastically lithe body rocking against me. In no time at all, all bets were off. The chips were down and I was up.

"Oh, Damon, Damon. . . ."

"Who, me?"

"Yes, you. I am willing to try to be a woman. I care no longer about the *Académie*. But can you give me what Mei Ling High gave me? Can you offer me the gates of true paradise as she did?"

"What are you talking about?"

She had her eyes closed, her red lips chewing into each other in unbridled ecstasy.

154

"Mei Ling High," she whispered, "placed me under the influence of hashish and then covered my body with roaming, moist tongues for a period of twenty-four hours! Do you know what that was like? Do you think any man could make me feel as she did? I became their slave, their tool, because of Mei Ling High. What man can equal burning lips and flaming drugs?"

"Try me," I urged. I added my weight to the urging.

"Lock the door then," she breathed fiercely, opening her eyes. "I'll show you how natural I truly am. I was born a redhead and I will die a redhead. I could have posed for Titian."

She was beginning to talk like a real woman now. I ran and bolted the door and got back to her before she started thinking about Mei Ling High again. It's this way with me. To hell with French jobs and hashish. I was convinced that one real sample of Damon and she'd be out of the Lesbian business forever. Lesbos are made, not born, same as everybody else.

Madame Lilly de Jussac was way ahead of me and not going anyplace. The leather skirt was off and she leaned back against one corner of the desk. Her smooth abdominal muscles undulated and bumped at me. She held out her long cool arms. Her green eyes glowed like a hungry cat's sizing up a nice fat sparrow.

"Come, Rod, my dear one," she murmured. "Let me see how you can make me forget Mei Ling High. Save me if you can, but I warn you, I still *like* girls. . . ."

"So who doesn't?" I laughed and shafted her where she stood. Coming in at forty-five degrees on a zing and a swear. She howled, in all her naked flaming glory, and enveloped me without batting an eye.

After that, it was off to the races and if you had asked her a long time later who Mei Ling High was she might have told you she never cared for Chinese food.

One thing about Madame Lilly de Jussac.

I've always admired a woman who's willing to learn.

There's always hope for *that* kind.

One thing more before I get back to my main interest in life. I had already made up my mind as to who my successor would be at the *Académie Sexualité* after I got my fill of the place. And the girls.

155

Brigitte Lebeau, of course.

There was one old dog who could teach all the young ones a whole new bag of tricks.

And then some.

My mind boggled when I thought of what Madame Brigitte's *Departmental* could and would be like.

Ooo-la-la-la!

Everything from soup to nuts.

And her idea of dessert would have to be in a class by itself.

But now I must draw the shade down on Madame Lilly de Jussac's sighs, screams and shouts of agony and sheer ecstasy.

I am also a gentleman, above all things.

Especially the ladies.

CHAPTER THIRTEEN

The peace talks had got no further when I took a night plane out of Orly Airport, but what the hell. At least the situation had a fair chance now without any busy little bodies to louse things up. I had done the job that Walrus-moustache and the Coxe Foundation had asked me to do. My assignment was over and closed and done. A success, on all counts.

There were a few tearful farewells which deserve passing mention. About Madame Brigitte Lebeau, I had no qualms and little to fear except fear itself. With the whole platoon of young willing ladies at the *Académie Sexualité* to keep her busy, she soon forgot about Rod Damon. Quite a warhorse, the Madame. She had already instituted some daring procedures as part of her curriculum for the school. I spied a Friday program that ommincluded the *Art Of Love In Five Special Stages*. The Madame demonstrated in the school auditorium with five willing male specimens from the French Academy of Athletes. I was sorry I couldn't stay to see the show. It must have been a gas, and those young ladies of the school had gotten more in one lesson from her than nine months with Madame Lilly de Jussac.

I took Mady Morrow on the town for one whole day and wound up with her in a private orgy atop the Eiffel Tower after the gates had closed and all visitors had left. A bribe to the elevator man didn't hurt at all. For a handful of francs, he disappeared and I endured some wonderful romping in the name of Sexual Research. Now I know what I am talking about when I discuss the Art Of Intercourse Seven Hundred Feet Above The Ground. It's the highest kind of flying and when Mady and I finally came down at three o'clock in the morning, staggering along the Left Bank for some fresh air, it was a dizzying sensation. Mady cried genuine tears when I bid her farewell but she understood.

"Golly, Damon, never a one like you!"

"You aren't so bad yourself, you blonde bomber."

"I can't thank you enough. I mean about telling me all about Yankowski and showing me all those tricks."

"You're a good woman and you deserved it. I take care of my girls."

She sighed and placed my right hand over her pulsating left breast. "See? Feel it?" There was plenty to see and plenty to feel.

"Sure. Your heart's beating. Congratulations. You're still alive."

"Dopy," she laughed happily. "Don't you understand? My heart hasn't beaten that way in years. You *woke* me up!"

"Then don't ever go back to sleep, Mady Morrow."

"I won't," she promised.

And I don't think she ever will.

My parting with Viviane Fresnay was a delicious, intimate, quiet, sturdy little romance. She'd managed to borrow a pal's pad on the *Rue de la Paix,* so we lived it up for a night. Viviane was all full of the French movie syndrome. *A Man And A Woman* and *The Umbrellas Of Cherbourg.* She was dreamy, enchanted, waltzed up with me and what I had, and the few hours we shared in a candlelit, *cafe espresso* atmosphere of love, passion and sex. What a charmer. If you wanted them all softness, curves and delectable femininity, the Vivianes of this world are the whole ball of wax. She could have won me forever were I not the sort of man I am—to whom variety is indeed the spice of life.

After a dozen explosions and collages of sex and fun, we said our goodbyes on a little bridge overlooking the Seine. She had stars in her eyes but she knew I was going. She put her arms around my waist as we both gazed down into the dirtiest water this side of the East River in New York.

"Rod, you are going back to America?"

"Tomorrow's first plane. I have to. You understand?"

"Of course. A man such as yourself must get back to all the other waiting ladies in the world." She sighed. "I will miss you. You have given me so much."

"You weren't exactly a miser either."

"I had much to give and you are a man who takes."

"Ain't it the truth?"

158

She smiled in the murky darkness of the night and pulled me toward her, and I came willingly. But she had obviously made her mind up about something already.

"*Adieu,* dear Rod," she murmured sadly and before I could stop her or cry for help, she put both hands against my chest and shoved. Back I went like the town drunk. And *down.* Into the dirty, gagging waters of the Seine. I never saw or heard Viviane Fresnay walking out of my life forever.

So it goes.

Win a few, lose a few.

And then the Last Goodbye was for Madame Lilly de Jussac.

It was a tryst with a twist. A date with a mate who had come a long, long way too. My women always emerge from associations with me as something different. A little better for it, I like to think, but you can never tell. You can't be too sure about anything in this day and age of spies, tricks and deceits.

She asked me to meet her at an address somewhere in the Rue de Pigalle. I went. I still had a half of a day left before I took wings and left Paris. My heart was happy and full. I was the cock of the walk. I had come, I had seen, I had conquered. The Paris of the postcards had become one of my finest hours. A true Damon pilgrimage down among the unschooled, ignorant women of the world.

Madame Lilly de Jussac opened the door of her darkened boudoir, invited me in and poured us a couple of cognacs.

She was naked, of course. For all my care and feeding of her soul, she had remained the true extrovert, the hopeless libertine.

"You will get naked," she commanded. "We have much to do."

"Honest?"

"Yes. I am hungry for you. Since that time in the office, I have experimented. With other men. I even paid a few husky boys from the grocers to consort with me. But—it is you I want. You who seem able to satisfy me. Is that all right with you?"

I was already down to my socks. The boudoir was a dim

dark place of invitation. I jumped into bed. Madame Lilly came around the other side. In the gloom, those splendid howitzers of hers trained down upon me. Her long wonderful body glowed dimly. I could hear her breathing. Soft and velvet-like. If you rubbed two pieces of velvet together, you would have gotten the same sound.

"Ready when you are, C.B."

"I am ready. I have stayed ready, Monsieur Rod."

She climbed into the bed, mounted me, trapped me with her gorgeous thighs and raised herself so that the divining stick was the very next thing she would feel. For a long moment, she held herself erect and then, like a dive-bomber plummeting On Target, she came down.

I kept my eyes open until she hit me.

Then I closed them.

Then I opened them again.

When the waves had hit her, she had transformed from a vengeful, sad pussycat to a true lioness and mate to the master of the pride.

Oh, yes, I cured Madame Lilly de Jussac. For all the time left to me, I scoured and cleansed her of sickness and cleared her mind for the finer things of life.

My last goodbye to her was the biggest hello in the books.

After all, I did have to catch a plane.

Also, there was somebody waiting for me in America.

Minda Loa.

With her feather, her tongue and her thesis.

Hell—isn't that the way this whole damn business started in the first place?